on the
RUN

a novel

William Shaw

Printed in the United States of America
First published in 2023 by Kilkenney Publishing.
Copyright © 2021 by William P. Shaw
Email: wpzshaw@gmail.com
ISBN 979-8-218-16879-7

Design and Typesetting: www.ebookscoversdesign.com

The author wishes to acknowledge and thank all those writers whose verse or prose is included in this book. Every effort has been made to contact the copyright holders of historical information included in this book. The publisher would welcome notice of any errors and omissions. This is a work of fiction. Names, characters, places, and incidents are the product of the author's imagination, Any resemblance to actual persons, living or dead, businesses, companies, events, or locales is entirely coincidental.

Permissions to print Seamus Heaney's "Follower" granted courtesy of Macmillan Publishing (U.S.) and Faber & Faber Ltd. (U.K., Commonwealth, and Canada). Permission to use the lyrics of "The Fields of Athenry" courtesy of Willow Branch Publishing.

To Connie: ". . . till the bluebells forget to bloom"

Follower

My father worked with a horse-plough,
His shoulders globed like a full sail strung
Between the shafts and the furrow.
The horse strained at his clicking tongue.

An expert. He would set the wing
And fit the bright steel-pointed sock.
The sod rolled over without breaking.
At the headrig, with a single pluck

Of reins, the sweating team turned round
And back into the land. His eye
Narrowed and angled at the ground,
Mapping the furrow exactly.

I stumbled in his hobnailed wake,
Fell sometimes on the polished sod;
Sometimes he rode me on his back
Dipping and rising to his plod.

I wanted to grow up and plough,
To close one eye, stiffen my arm.
All I ever did was follow
In his broad shadow round the farm.

I was a nuisance, tripping, falling,
Yapping always. But today
It is my father who keeps stumbling
Behind me, and will not go away.

– Seamus Heaney (from *100 Poems*)

Prologue

IN THE FADING LIGHT, FAR BELOW the heights of Classiebawn Castle, sea gatherers negotiated the slick, rocky descent from Mullaghmore's cliffs to the sandy beach below, where land and sea collided, often with merciless enmity. As always, *eadails* from the ocean beckoned the local gatherers—logs and planks, barrels, and rafts off the decks of ships at sea; remnants of cargo including bales of rubber, driftwood, a block of tallow, and on the rare occasion a cask of whiskey. The ocean teased the villagers endlessly with food and bounty, but at fierce risk to their lives. Bred in the bone of every gatherer was the knowledge that if you misread the ocean's mood, the deep would rise to claim you.

Classiebawn brooded blindly atop the cliff called Fairy Rock this late-August evening, 1979. Lord Palmerston, twice Prime Minister of Britain, had built this large, turreted, cyclopean castle in the shadow of Ben Bulben in the mid-nineteenth century, as much to notarize Britain's long ascendancy in Ireland as to glorify himself. Palmerston was deeply reviled in Ireland for his wholesale famine evictions and for the great wealth he amassed building the infamous "coffin ships."

The current owner of Classiebawn, Queen Victoria's great-grandson, the famous Lord Mountbatten, was present for his annual summer holiday. Mountbatten, unlike Palmerston, had a reputation for being friendly to the Irish, and many returned that

1

good feeling. However, this being the smoldering tenth year of the Troubles, many did not.

In the half light, several hundred meters from the gatherers, two men in scuba gear and backpacks, entered the harborside waters below Classiebawn. They swam stealthily toward a twenty-eight-foot fishing boat—the *Shadow V*. Working quickly under water, they attached five pounds of gelignite to the bottom of the craft and affixed a timing device. Then they swam back to shore, removed their gear, and placed it in their backpacks. One of the men shone a flashlight toward the top of the cliff. A third man returned the flash from the heights, then drove his car to the harbor, retrieved the two divers, and sped into the darkness.

Chapter One

A SLIVER OF LIGHT SEPARATED THE OCEAN from the darkening pink-blue sky on the horizon as Terence Connolly stepped outside his whitewashed cottage, placed two calloused fingers in his mouth, and whistled for his son, Tim. His high-pitched signal pierced the air like a lightning shaft and echoed through the grassy, tree-shorn hills behind the cottage. It was suppertime.

Bridget, Terence's slender, auburn-haired, thirty-eight-year-old wife, was cleaning the flounder he'd caught that morning, a white cotton apron covering her beige, ankle-length house dress. This night was special. Terence's grandfather, Brian Connolly, had just arrived from Cork. Advancing age made his trips to coastal Mullaghmore less frequent, but since he hadn't visited Sligo in two years, he was looking forward to a relaxing late summer visit and a chance to tell some of his favorite stories to young Tim.

Tim had been tending the sheep two kilometers from the cottage when Brian arrived. Hearing his father's whistle, the fourteen-year-old signaled his border collie, Millie, to herd the sheep to the adjoining field. He pulled his woolen cap down tight over his long, red hair, then set off at full speed, his wiry body weaving down the hill, leaping over rivulets, hurdling low stone fences, skirting thorny patches of yellow gorse, deftly dodging field patties left by their sheep and their few cows.

The boy loved this part of the day, the running part, the part where the day's chores were done and he was free, free to ramble up and down the hills, imagining that one afternoon a sea-borne breeze would lift him among the seagulls, soaring high above the green-gray tapestry of field, stone, and sea below him. He would dip and glide, alone and weightless.

This evening, Tim's footfall was even more rapid. He was looking forward to the rare visit from the old man. His great-grandfather was not only the repository of family history, he was also the family's *shanachie*, specializing in tales of faeries, ghosts, deadly portents, and mortal terror.

###

Bushy bearded, bald, and marked by a four-inch scar on his left cheek, seventy-eight-year-old Brian was the family's legendary rebel, or rather the latest in a line of Connolly rebels.

His grandfather, Ambrose Connolly, had been a child in 1849 when their landlord's agent, Charles Griffith, Esquire, sent the constable to cast the family into the streets to starve and die. As a young man, Ambrose joined the Fenian Uprising in Cork; he was one of four thousand rebels who marched to the Limerick train junction, attacking and burning a string of Royal Constabulary barracks in their path.

Brian's own father, Padraig, joined a group of Fenians impatient with the "shunning" tactics of Michael Davitt's Land League boycotts. Padraig's Fenians burned landlords' crops, maimed their cattle, and in some cases, murdered the landlords themselves. During the War of Independence, young Brian and his brother fought side by side against the Black and Tans from 1919 to 1921. After his brother, the first Tim, was killed during an ambush in West Cork, Brian joined General Liam "Billy" Pilkington in Sligo but was captured during an attack on a Royal Irish Constabulary barracks. He spent six months in prison and was released when the treaty was signed.

###

Tim arrived at the front door breathless and smiling, his heavy gray cotton shirt stained with sweat under his arms and his wide suspenders. After greeting his parents and his great-grandfather, he went to the bathroom to wash his hands and face.

The bathroom was the Connolly's primary concession to the twentieth century. Although the cottage had been in the family for four generations, only a mere ten years ago had Terence added an extension to the back of the cottage, then installed indoor plumbing.

That was what Terence did—he built things. He'd thatched his own roof, a twelve-inch-thick, neatly woven masterpiece. He'd mastered the essential skills of the Sligo farmer: building towering haystacks called "trampcocks," slicing turf, herding sheep and cattle, harvesting seaweed, fishing in the tolerable weather, and weaving fish nets during the dark winter months.

The Connolly cottage itself had three bedrooms and a kitchen/living area with a large fireplace. The rear of the house faced the ocean and was windowless, built to fend off the punishing wind and rain, while the front faced east, looking out at the hills and meadows. Three small windows, one in the kitchen and one in each of the bedrooms on either side, provided light and panoramic views of their spacious farm. Red and yellow rose bushes and wild, fluffy blue sheep's-bit brightened the perimeter of the cottage.

Bridget still cooked dinners in the hearth, the same hearth that warmed the house in the winter and chased the Atlantic's nightly chill in the summer. Blackened cast-iron three-legged pots, plus a kettle and a teapot, stood like dutiful sentinels on either side of the fireplace. In the corner of the kitchen, a wooden dresser displayed delft mugs, bowls, and other blue-patterned ironstone plates and serving dishes.

Tonight, after the family devoured every morsel of the baked flounder fillets, boiled buttered potatoes, and cabbage with chunks of ham, Bridget cleared the table. Then, once the sun had set, Terence set a blazing fire of turf and cherrywood. As the firelight shadows danced on the kitchen wall, Bridget wrapped a shaggy, pilled woolen shawl around her shoulders and joined the family circle near the hearth for Brian's tales.

The grizzly-bearded grandfather adjusted the knot in his tie and pulled his worn tweed jacket tighter to his chest. He began his storytelling as always, in a deep, tremulous voice, swearing to God or on his dear mother's grave that these stories were "absolutely true."

For the next two hours, Brian mesmerized Tim and amused Terence and Bridget with tales of local Irishmen who battled vengeful ghosts in the hoary forests, usually but not always escaping capture and certain death. He also told tales of nocturnal child-stealing faeries and—most disturbingly—tales of banshees whose wailing in the night foreshadowed imminent death.

This night, Brian told two such tales. The first recalled a banshee with streaming red hair, a ghastly green complexion, and eyes that were dark red from her continual weeping. This banshee's wailing foretold the imprisonment and death of a beloved family member, far away from home and far beyond the family's anguished efforts to save him. The second, even more terrifying tale, described three banshees whose bloodcurdling screams throughout the night signaled the grisly death of someone great or holy.

Chapter Two

EARLY THE NEXT MORNING, AUGUST 27, 1979, a cloudless blue sky greeted Terence and Tim as they hitched their ass, Zeus, to the broad rake. It was time to gather the handshakings of hay in the fields just north of Classiebawn. Most of the summer's hay labor had been done—picking the weeds, shaking and loosening the hay, and preparing the lappings and rucks for the bad weather. Now the hay was dry enough to build the trampcocks.

Tim's task was to lead Zeus through the handshakings, pulling them to the building site. Once the boy gathered the hay, Terence prepared the foundation for the trampcock. Tim's next task was to fork the loose hay to his father. Terence built and shaped his tower, layer after layer. He laid the outside wads of hay clockwise in a circle, tied them on the inside, and then tramped them solid. He was careful to let out the sides at just the right time, then take them in just as carefully when the trampcock was high enough.

When he completed the foundation, Terence pulled it around, then combed and shaped the sides with the rake, repeating this process until he chose a final lapping of hay for the top. This done, he tied it down with hay ropes. With the first stack finished, Terence slid down, put his arm around Tim's shoulder, and surveyed his handiwork.

"Time for our break, lad."

The father and son had finished their first trampcock of the day in good time and now greeted Bridget near the cliff's edge, where she, as usual, was waiting for them with two cups and a can of tea covered with a sock to keep it hot. As her long, auburn hair lifted with the light breeze, she handed them a napkin-covered basket with thick slices of brown bread, fresh from the oven, moistened with chunks of melted butter. Millie wagged her tail, begging for a chunk of bread. When Tim tore off a small piece and tossed it to her, the dog leapt two feet into the air to catch it.

While savoring their snack, Bridget, Terence, and Tim recounted some of Brian's ghoulish tales and venerable superstitions from the previous evening. Bridget thought they were darker, more disturbing than the tales he had told in the past. Terence agreed, joking that the old man was not mellowing with age. Tim, on the other hand, had enjoyed every minute of the storytelling. He said it was like "living in the middle of a horror movie."

After fifteen minutes, Bridget gathered the basket and napkins and kissed her "boys" before returning to the cottage, Millie scampering at her heels through scattered patches of lacy white meadowsweet.

Before they set back to work, Terence stood and stretched his arms and his back, readying himself for the next trampcock. Tim sat for one last moment and took stock of the glorious day. In front of him, the wild Atlantic Ocean rushed in, relentlessly scouring the jagged stones below. Over his left shoulder, the grand castle stood like the gnomon of a sundial. Beyond the castle, the massive, wrinkled brow of Ben Bulben silently acknowledged everything below, peering down like some wizened, inscrutable sage. Flowering, violet-blue spring-squill dotted the coastal grasslands. Scattered willow trees on the field's edge allowed their branches to sway with the soft breeze.

As Terence glanced over the cliff, he detected movement in the harbor and recognized *Shadow V*—the Earl Mountbatten's fishing boat—leaving the harbor. He pointed out Mountbatten and his family to Tim as the green boat chugged smoothly toward the lobster pot markers outside the Red Island, which locals called "Oilean Ruadh." It was a scene of transcendent calm and beauty.

Suddenly, a thunderous, ear-clapping explosion shattered the peace. Tim and Terence ran back from the cliff's edge, recoiling in fear and horror.

"Jaysus Christ Almighty!" shrieked Terence, bug-eyed and trembling. Tim, terrified, staggered back over to the cliff's edge.

"Da!" screamed the terrified boy, pointing in the direction of the blast. Below them, fragments of boat, clothing, and shattered bodies bobbed in the water, while splintered remnants of wood, bone, and flesh were still floating windborne, to the surface of the water. After several moments of silent shock, people below scattered, running and screaming in terror and confusion. Within minutes, Gardai and hospital sirens filled the air. Mullaghmore's bucolic paradise had suddenly transmogrified into a sorrowful inferno.

"Provos," said Terence in a trembling voice. "Bloody hell. Let's get out of here, son. We'll finish all this another day."

Chapter Three

TERENCE AND BRIDGET TENDED THEIR CHORES in a sullen haze for two days. Bridget herself had attended a prayer service at the harbor with fifty or more neighbors the day after the explosion, where she'd been appalled to discover that a local fourteen-year-old boy, Paul Maxwell, had been killed in the blast along with his friend, Nicholas, one of Mountbatten's twin grandsons. Bridget knew that Paul was a school chum of Tim's. She was terrified to imagine that her son might be at risk as well now that this once-peaceful enclave had become a war zone, a fearful place for old and young.

Brian, on the other hand, wrestled with a range of emotions. He vented continuously about the explosion, one moment cursing the Brits for bringing this on themselves, another moment fearing the reprisals and the setbacks the Republic would suffer. Then he expressed pity, pity since the explosion killed not only Mountbatten, whom Brian called "a decent bloke," but also his wife, his grandson, and the young Paul Maxwell. With all this, Mullaghmore itself was now under siege. The Gardai, government troops, and undercover agents descended like a biblical plague on the village and set up an operations center in "The Pier Head Hotel." They immediately cordoned off the crime scene and began combing the beach, the shoreline, and the cliffs, gathering any available evidence, interviewing witnesses, and canvassing all nearby homes. Their number more than doubled when the reporters arrived.

The responsible party was not in doubt—the IRA had brazenly claimed responsibility, not only for the attack on Mountbatten, but also for the killing, hours later, of eighteen British soldiers in two booby-trap bomb explosions in County Down. But here, the assassination of a prominent member of Britain's royal family, the queen's cousin, blotted out all else. This was worldwide news, and the search for the actual bombers assumed a frenzied importance.

Public opinion divided Sligo residents, especially in Mullaghmore. Many thought it was past time to "get tough" with their historic enemies. Others thought the murder of a seventy-nine-year-old grandfather was a senselessly brutal and cowardly act. Others still were further outraged that the killers had violated his honored status as a guest. And, of course, innocent children were also killed.

A spokesman for the IRA, however, called Mountbatten's killing "an execution"—"a discriminate act to bring to the attention of the British people the continuing occupation of our country." He said this act should be seen "in contrast to the apathy of the British Government and English people to the deaths of over three hundred British soldiers and the deaths of Irish men, women, and children at the hands of their forces."

Responding to the assassination, newly elected prime minister Margaret Thatcher called the IRA a criminal rather than a political organization and withdrew from IRA prisoners the political rights associated with prisoner-of-war status.

Amidst the chaos enveloping them, Terence, Bridget, and Tim attended to their necessary chores, but in a tense, fearful, and altered environment. Because of their proximity to the scene of the crime, the authorities twice interviewed Terence and Bridget to inquire what they might have heard or seen in the days before, as well as since, the blast. During a second visit, one senior officer took special note of Brian's presence and wryly commented on his enduring reputation as a Fenian hero in the west and south of Ireland, surprised he was even still alive. Brian himself said nothing, scowling and scarcely acknowledging his presence. However, he decided it was time now to leave Mullaghmore and return to Cork. This constant presence of police and the small army of investigators was wearing on his nerves, scraping old wounds and grievances.

Brian Connolly had earned his reputation and his four-inch scar in West Cork's legendary ambush at Kilmichael in November 1921. He was one of the thirty-six members of Tom Barry's flying column that ambushed a section of the Auxiliary Division police. These British "Auxies," tough veterans of the First World War, had been brutally successful in their efforts to stanch the rebellion.

Barry's plan was audacious, considered foolhardy by many, since his ambush was staged on a road running through marshy land and bordered by large clumps of rock where there was no line of retreat. Brian knew this was not a hit-and-run attack. It was a fight-to-the-death attack.

He and his squad concealed themselves in the rocky hills, close to the side of the road. Brian would always remember the discomfort of that battle—holding their positions through the rainy night, soaking wet and chilled to the bone, waiting hours for the enemy convoy. When the first lorry finally arrived, Tom Barry threw a grenade into the cab, and the hidden riflemen opened fire at close range. The Auxies in the first lorry were immediately killed. Those in the second lorry were able to return fire with rifles and pistols before engaging in grisly hand-to-hand combat. Brian himself emptied his rifle, then used his bayonet and even his rifle butt in the close quarters, taking a bloody slash to the side of his face. As one Auxie stood up to surrender, Brian's brother, Tim, went to accept his surrender. The Auxie, however, pulled a pistol and shot him between the eyes. Brian screamed, picked up a dead soldier's rifle, and emptied the cartridge into the Auxie's head.

Tom Barry then sent out the word. "No surrenders. Keep firing at them." No British soldiers survived the ambush.

Chapter Four

IT WAS THREE YEARS AFTER THE ATTACK before Brian Connolly returned to Mullaghmore, though Terence and his family visited the old man in Cork several times in the interim. Late spring and summer were the best times to travel south, given the longer hours of daylight and warmer weather. Bridget enjoyed shopping and wandering about Cork's abundant "English Market." Terence and Tim usually joined Brian for a hurling match. They even watched the exciting Cork vs. Sligo match in 1981, which Cork, a perennial powerhouse, won in overtime.

One Sunday afternoon, Brian took Terence and Tim to a "road bowling" competition on a nearby country road. Brian explained to his great-grandson how the thrower would run to a chalk line, lift his arm and the steel ball up and back, then whirl downward into an underhand throw, releasing the bowl before stepping over the mark. The rules stated that wherever the steel ball stopped, another chalk mark was made, and the next throw was taken from behind that mark. The winner was determined by the person or team able to reach a predetermined location with the fewest throws. Brian mentioned that he enjoyed the sport and had bowled for many years himself after moving to Cork. Terence laughingly informed Tim that his great-grandfather had been banned from the sport some years ago after beaning a competitor with an errant toss. The wounded bowler accused Brian of doing it deliberately.

Brian didn't deny it. He simply grinned. "He was a liar, a cheater and a horse's arse. He deserved it. Besides 'twas only a glancing blow. A bull's eye would've done him in for sure."

Finally, on December 4, 1982, Brian returned to Mullaghmore for Tim's seventeenth birthday. Tim had added weight and height since the old man's last visit, though he was still two inches shy of his father's six feet. He wore his red hair longer now, almost down to his shoulders. Now in the third year of his Senior Cycle, Tim was a good student and looked forward to studying Agricultural Science at UC Galway. However, since he worked long hours each week helping with the farm, Tim had no social life. He was shy around the girls. He didn't drink or smoke. Consequently, he also didn't associate with the local lads, who spent their idle hours bragging about local lasses they shagged, or lying about their plans to join the IRA, while they smoked their fags and guzzled beers on the beach or kicked the ball around the local pitch. They considered Tim an outsider, an oddball, maybe even a bit "thick." They never bothered or bullied him, however. His father's reputation as a quiet and friendly man was mediated by local memory of his violent outbursts on the pitch, where his antagonists had always fared poorly. The other boys wanted no part of him or his family.

After a night of storytelling and singing of old ballads, Brian took to bed early, knackered from his long trip. The next morning, Terence borrowed his friend Jimmy McKee's thirty-three-foot, 130-horsepower Mermaid Marine Engine Aqua Star in exchange for some of the fish they might catch.

They'd picked a perfect late-autumn day. The sky was clear but for a few wispy clouds. With the water calm, the trip out to

Donegal Bay was serene, though gloriously disturbed by several humpback whale and dolphin sightings.

Tim manned the boat's sonar and suggested they drop anchor at a promising site, about five nautical miles offshore. Brian sat back, soaking in the sun, the chill air, and the scenery, while Bridget, Terence, and Tim cast their lines overboard. Within three hours, Bridget had caught two Mackerel, one Cod, and one Whiting, besting Terence's two Pollock and Tim's single Mackerel and Cod. They cleaned the fish on board, put them on ice in a Styrofoam chest, and threw the offal to the trailing seals and hovering gulls.

Once back at the cottage, after resting, dining, and singing "Happy Birthday" to Tim, Terence and Brian walked Millie behind the house as the sun was slipping into the ocean. Brian lit a cigarette.

"I love this place, Grandfather," Terence said wistfully as he scanned the landscape with its bare, rolling hills and rambling patches of purple rhododendron. He threw back his head and inhaled the briny air. "It's my piece of heaven." He paused, picked up a stick, and threw it. Millie rushed to retrieve it. "But . . . these are some bloody painful times." Terence took the retrieved stick from Millie's mouth and threw it again. "I keep hoping for some relief from the bombs and the killings, but, as you said once, it never feckin ends."

"My experience," said Brian, "has ill fitted me for optimism, lad. It will likely get worse, especially given the ruthless nature of that hoor Thatcher and the ruthless nature of the bombers." The old man paused, took a last drag off his cigarette, dropped it, and crushed it with his foot. "It's sad to see the changes in Mullaghmore since the assassination. The bloody graffiti fouling the walls by the pier . . ." He shook his head.

Terence knelt to scratch Millie's belly, and she stretched and groaned with delight. Looking up at his grandfather, Terence told him how reporters from print and TV media had continued to snoop around the village, especially on the anniversaries of the assassination. "They still visit the hotel and guesthouses, all of them eager to make a name for themselves looking for some new angle on the bombing."

Terence complained that the relentless probing was preventing the wound from healing. It was feeding neighbors' divided feelings, widening fissures that might otherwise have disappeared with time. Was the assassination warranted or unwarranted? Was it a strong statement for the Republic, or a cowardly deed? Would it damage Ireland in the face of the world, hurt an already struggling economy, keep needed industry from coming to her shores and fueling growth?

Together, Terence and Brian gnawed on this bone for another hour.

Chapter Five

TWO MORNINGS LATER, BRIAN PACKED his bag to catch the nine-thirty bus to Enniskillen. The old man had planned a trip across the border for a reunion with two surviving friends from the war. This might well be their last chance to rehash the adventures of their youth.

He planned to catch the bus by the harbor, but Terence insisted that he would drive his grandfather the seventy kilometers into the Northern town. They set out after breakfast. Bridget prepared bag lunches for Terence and Brian, then gave Brian a warm embrace at the front door. Brian shook Tim's shoulders, telling him that he was a fine young man and would make his family and country proud someday.

Tim felt sad to see the wild old man leave.

Terence, meanwhile, kissed Bridget on the cheek and told her he would be home for dinner. He tousled his son's hair, grabbed his shoulder, and playfully pulled him to his chest. Then he got behind the wheel, and they drove off.

After an hour on the N 16, as Terence approached the border town of Belcoo, he spotted a traffic jam ahead. Cars formed a long queue as British soldiers brandishing assault rifles, wearing helmets and body armor, stopped and searched each car and questioned motorists. Terence and Brian waited for twenty minutes until a tall thin soldier approached and asked for his driver's license.

When he saw "Mullaghmore" on Terence's license, he baited

him with questions. "So, Mister Connolly, are ye in sympathy with the bloody murderers who killed the Lord Mountbatten and his family three years ago? Are ye some Fenian cunt like them?"

"Just a peaceful citizen," said Terence, sensing danger. "No need for the harsh attitude, Corporal." The soldier curled his lip in contempt and returned Terence's license. A second soldier approached the passenger side of the car and took the credentials Brian handed him for inspection. Brian, unconcerned, chewed his ham sandwich, unaware that a fleck of mayonnaise-coated lettuce rested in his beard. The soldier scanned Brian's papers with unexpected interest.

"Mr. Brian Connolly," said the soldier. "We have your name on our list—an ancient murdering rebel and a former guest of the Crown, who we also know happens to be on his way to meet a group of his old IRA comrades."

"No law against that now, is there, laddie?" Brian chuckled.

"These are tough times now Mr. Connolly," the soldier replied. "Laws ain't what they used to be. Certainly on this side of the border. Get out of the car, please," he demanded.

"Get out of the car, me arse," said Brian. "I'm an old man eatin' his lunch. I'm sure as hell no threat to anyone. So bugger off. Get out of the feckin way and let us be."

"That's quite enough of that lip, ye old bastard." The soldier opened the door, grabbed the old man's arm, and dragged him out of the car.

"Get yer bloody hands off him!" Terence shouted. "He's done nothin."

He tried to get out of the car, but the thin soldier held the door shut. In response, Terence violently pushed the door and the soldier away from the door. When the soldier came at him with his rifle butt, Terence dodged to his left, then smashed the right side of the soldier's head with a vicious left hook, staggering him. As three other soldiers came running from the roadblock, Terence punched another one, then turned to help his grandfather, only to be hit in the face by a third soldier's rifle butt, knocking him dizzy and bloody mouthed to the ground. Two soldiers then took turns kicking him in the back, the stomach, and the head as he tried in vain to cover himself. Brian struggled to help his grandson, but the replacements quickly restrained him.

Both men were summarily arrested, placed in a police van, and settled in a local holding cell, where they were propped in steel chairs with their hands cuffed behind their backs. The two soldiers struck by Terence took turns punching his face and beating his shins and ribs with their batons throughout the day. Brian, seething with anger, was forced to watch his grandson endure this abuse, while even he received several blows to the head and legs himself. Secured in handcuffs and leg irons, they stepped onto an army bus and were transferred to Belfast's Maze Prison the next morning, December 6.

Chapter Six

THE SURF CHURNED RAGGEDLY on this dark windy day, five weeks after Terence's arrest. Waves tirelessly thrashed the flat stones below the cliffs. A light salt spray scented the air, and a brisk wind blew Tim's hair around his face as he and Bridget left their cottage for the short trek into town.

Mother and son walked in silence toward the village square. Millie trotted a few feet in front of them. Tim's faded black woolen jacket was zipped up, the collar tight around his neck. Reaching the town square, they stood at the bus stop outside the Quay Restaurant and Pub.

Bridget took Tim's hand. "This will only be for a short while, son. We'll sort all this, and ye'll be back with us as soon as possible."

"I don't want to go, Ma," said Tim. "I should stay here and help ye with the chores. I don't want to go."

"We've been over this, Timmy. I'll manage sure enough," said Bridget, unconvincingly. "I need to find some work, and I'll need time to visit with Da. Most of all, I need ye away from the local IRA fellas, especially after what happened to poor Paul Maxwell and his poor heartbroken family. Some of these young Provos have already been stirring local anger over Da's arrest, and I heard that one or two of their lads have approached ye. That cannot happen, son. I want ye to be safe, and I want ye to finish yer schoolin'." Bridget's voiced cracked, and and as her eyes welled with tears, she dabbed at them with her sleeve. "Ye'll be safe with your Aunt Mary and Uncle Gary, and ye can come home as soon as Da comes home." Her hair lifted gently from the uncovered back of her kerchief as she spoke.

Tim nodded and whispered doubtfully, "Yeah, Ma." He stared at the ground, his face a mask pinched between sorrow and anger.

When the battered, exhaust-belching bus wheezed into the harbor square, Bridget embraced her son, her face taut and misty-eyed. She forced a smile and told Tim to be polite and obedient to his aunt and uncle. The young man nodded, then stepped into the bus, walked to the rear, tossed his small bag on the seat, and peered out the back window. As the bus to Shannon Airport pulled away, Tim stared blankly at his mother and pressed his hand to the window. Millie chased the bus for about two hundred meters before returning to the weeping woman, as she clutched her heavy sweater over her wash-worn cotton house dress against the chill Atlantic wind.

Chapter Seven

SHORTLY AFTER THE AER LINGUS 747 whooshed, squealed, and rattled down the Kennedy runway, Tim entered the vast terminal and joined hundreds of weary travelers crammed into roped pathways, snaking slowly through customs. As he waited for an available customs officer, he fidgeted nervously, raising himself up and down on his toes.

After clearing customs, Tim took the exit ramp into the terminal, scanning the blur of human movement. Dozens of bored-looking men in dark suits and caps held cardboard signs with printed surnames. Waves of faceless people whirled around him as though trapping him in some phantasmagoria. Suddenly, his mother's sister, Mary Laherty, emerged as out of a thick fog. A plump, sweet-faced, smiling woman with sad blue eyes, Mary had short curly hair, the same auburn shade as Bridget's. The family resemblance was obvious, though she was several inches shorter and two years' younger than Bridget. She called his name and waved to him.

Relieved, Tim returned the wave. When she reached him, she gave him a warm embrace. Tim's arms hung lifelessly at his side. Mary held his shoulders, then stepped back to look at him.

"Ah, Tim, you've grown so tall, lad, since last I've seen ye." Her Sligo accent was unmolested by her years in America. "What is it? Four years?"

"Yes, ma'am," he said.

"Well, ye look grand. Let's be getting your luggage," Mary said.

"I've got it!" Tim held up his black bag. Mary seemed surprised, then just shrugged her shoulders.

"We'll be off then."

It took them another half hour to negotiate the noisy, crowded terminal, catch the shuttle bus to the parking garage, then find the right elevator to the right floor, to the right aisle, and the right letter space occupied by Mary's scuffed blue 1965 Chevy sedan. They escaped the confusion of the airport in time to encounter the Belt Parkway's heavy midday traffic. The city noise rattled Tim's jet-lag torpor. He stared sleepy-eyed through the Chevy's window, taking in the sights and sounds of New York. Twenty feet from Mary's crawling car, four dark-skinned guys with hooded sweatshirts and pulsating power tools were field stripping a disabled vehicle, rapidly tossing the tires and other removable parts onto their flatbed truck.

Three hours after arriving at Mary and her husband Gary's spare, two-bedroom Elmhurst apartment above Rudy's Delicatessen, Tim sat down in their cramped, tidy kitchen for his first meal in America. The three shared a bucket of fried chicken with coleslaw and biscuits. Gary, a trim, fit, humorless man, wiped his hands and mouth with a paper napkin, quietly sipping from his cup of tea. He still wore the starched white dress shirt and navy-blue tie of his FDNY dress uniform. Gary had attended the funeral of a fellow firefighter earlier in the day, and he was in a somber mood. His navy-blue jacket, replete with service ribbons, lay folded neatly over the empty kitchen chair. At the moment, however, he was assessing this new event in his life, and this new person, with uncertainty and chagrin. He leaned back in his chair and ran his fingers through his neatly trimmed, salt-and-pepper hair.

###

Gary was fourth-generation Irish. His great-grandfather, William Laherty, had arrived in New York in December 1847, one of four children his father Patrick had booked on the Edgar *out of Liverpool, specifically to save them from the famine raging through Kilkenney. The Laherty children joined scores of famine escapees in Manhattan's "Hell's Kitchen."*

The dreadful density of the impoverished Irish population in Hell's Kitchen had the one salutary effect of keeping the famine Irish in touch with their folkways, as did the churches and schools they attended, and the fiercely tribal manner in which they celebrated their holidays, baptisms, weddings, and funerals. Gary's family resembled many Irish families in New York that worked their way into the middle class. They secured civil service jobs with the police or fire departments; they worked as politicians, bartenders, restaurant owners, or priests and nuns. And they looked out for one another. Additionally, organizations like the Ancient Order of the Hibernians, scattered throughout the metropolitan area, zealously promoted all things Irish.

One Hibernian chapter, in fact, made it possible for young Gary Laherty to meet young Mary Walsh. After his graduation from Bishop Loughlin High School in 1949, Gary and his family joined a Hibernian-sponsored tour of Ireland. The tour group spent the last four nights of the trip in a small Sligo village. Ostensibly, the goal was to visit the cultural and historical landmarks associated with W. B. Yeats and his circle, along with the many prehistoric burial sites associated with Celtic history. Their arrival also coincided with the popular five-day August Fair in Tubbercurry, an annual festival of horse and cattle trading, pub crawls, traditional music sessions, and demonstrations of thatching, weaving, and threshing.

What most piqued Gary's interest, however, was the number of pretty girls he had seen at the fair. And since a talent and beauty contest was a highlight of the week, Gary convinced himself and his parents that attending this event constituted a significant cultural experience.

Mary Walsh and her taller, older sister, Bridget, were two of the twelve contestants who took the stage in traditional green woolen dresses; each featured an ornamental Celtic design on the tightly fitted bodice and a short skirt that flared from the waist to just above the knees. Knee-length socks and shiny black shoes finished the ensemble. Each contestant would either sing a song, or recite a poem in Irish, or they would step dance to the accompaniment of a flute, tin whistle, or accordion. Bridget danced a jig and a hornpipe with expert foot clacking and high kicking, arms stiff at her sides. Mary sang a soulfully beautiful rendition of the "Fields of Athenry" to guitar, flute, and banjo accompaniment. Mary won the contest and Gary's heart. He approached her nervously after the event, and she greeted him just as nervously. They fell in love quickly, though, and over the next few days were inseparable.

Gary was heartbroken to leave Sligo and Mary at the end of the tour. They wrote frequently and ardently to each other over the next two years.

After Gary passed his civil service exam, but before he began his assignment with the Fire Department of New York, he returned to Sligo with the express purpose of marrying Mary. He proposed to her in dramatic fashion, kneeling at the foot of the ancient burial mound on the top of Knocknarea, and she accepted. They married in

Tubbercurry's Church of St. John. It was a sad parting for Mary and her family when she left Ireland to live with Gary in New York, but her love for him allowed her to leave the green fields of Sligo for the gray streets of Queens.

They had a son thirteen months after they arrived in New York. Martin Laherty was their only child, and they were desolate when he was killed in a mortar attack three days before the fall of Saigon in 1975. He was only twenty-two years old.

Gary pressed his lips together and tapped the fingertips of his left hand on the kitchen table. He labored to engage Tim in conversation.

"So, how're your folks?" he asked. Mary threw Gary an angry look, pressed her lips, and shook her head. Gary shrugged, looking puzzled. "What? It's a normal question."

Tim rested a half-eaten chicken thigh on his plate and answered. "Ma's doin okay, I'd say. The prison authorities haven't let her see me Da yet. They say she may be able to visit him soon, but only once or twice a month."

"And your father?" Gary asked.

"Don't know," Tim said. "Not sure how long they plan to hold him."

The man got up and took a toothpick from the cupboard. Holding it in hand, he questioned Tim about his father's motives.

"What was he thinking?" Gary inquired.

Tim shrugged his shoulders and shook his head wearily. He was about to respond when Mary urged her husband, "Please, love, stop badgering the lad."

Gary clumsily changed the subject and reminded Tim that he was expected to "carry his weight with chores and errands."

Tim said, "Yes, sir. Ma gave me strict orders."

"Well then, Tim, you'll be wanting yer rest," Mary said. "Ye've a big day tomorrow. I'm so happy we were able to get ye here just as the second semester of the school year is beginning. We think you'll like St. Jude's. Martin certainly did. Gary's cleared some space in Martin's closet and chest of drawers for ye."

Tim offered a weary, dispirited nod. "Good night to ye, then. Thanks for the fine meal."

In the living room, Gary waited until Tim's door closed. He looked at Mary and raised his arms.

"One bag?" he whispered. "What the hell! Are we supposed to clothe him as well as feed, house, and school him?"

"Shhhh!" Mary whispered, struggling to keep peace and quell her own doubts at the same time. "I'm sorry, me love. Please don't be too tough on the lad. He has nothing. Worse now, away from home. With God's help, things will improve, and he'll be here only a short while."

"And I don't like him in Marty's room," Gary said, ignoring her.

"Merciful God, Gary. He's Marty's cousin. He's not some stranger."

He pressed his lips together, then shook his head. Rubbing his face with his hands, he let out a deep sigh. Mary walked behind him and put her arms around his neck to console him. "Him sleeping there will not bring Marty back," she continued. "The poor lad needs help. Bridget cannot afford to keep him now. She has almost no income, and she needs to travel some distance to visit her Terence whenever she gets a chance." Mary gently rubbed Gary's cheek. "And she was afraid for the lad. IRA men are always after recruiting the local boys. She doesn't want him in trouble like his Da now. He'll be safe here."

Tim's bedroom was clean and staged like a museum diorama. Four photographs of his cousin stood like altar pieces on the bedroom dresser: Marty as a two-year old, Marty as a Little Leaguer, Marty as a high school graduate, Marty as an Army sergeant. The Army photo had a Silver Star, a Purple Heart, and a black swatch draped over it. Three framed photographs decorated the sidewall: one of rotund Pope John XXIII, one of John F. Kennedy, and one of a blue-eyed, handsomely coiffed Jesus Christ pointing to his exposed heart with his left hand, while the first two fingers of his right hand pointed heavenward. Boy's clothes, baseball catcher's gear, a basketball, a hockey stick, football pads, and a deflated football crammed the closet. And Martin's army uniform.

Tim stripped to his underwear, threw his clothes on a chair, then lay down on the bed. The tense whispers from the outer room exacerbated his increasing desolation. He stared at the ceiling, restlessly replaying the last few tumultuous weeks of his life, until merciful sleep took him away.

Chapter Eight

BRIDGET RETURNED TO HER COTTAGE after Tim's departure. She threw several turf bricks on the fire, wrapped her shawl around her shoulders, and sat in her rocking chair, numb.

Millie jumped into her lap, and Bridget petted her aimlessly. Her mind was a blank space. She thought it strange that she couldn't feel anything. Was there something wrong with her? She thought about chores that needed attention. Dishes in the sink from this morning's breakfast had to be washed and dried. The laundry basket was filled with clothes—hers and Tim's. Her bedroom hadn't been swept, and the bathroom hadn't been scrubbed since Terence left the house weeks earlier. Tim's bed hadn't been made.

And what about the animals? Tim had been herding the sheep and feeding the cattle. She would have to take care of that. When? Now? Maybe tomorrow. Supper. What about supper? Lamb stew in the fridge. She thought about eating it, but she wasn't hungry.

The last few weeks without Terence had been unbearable. Alone in her bed, she often slipped over to his space in the middle of the night, half expecting him to be there, only to feel a searing pain when he was not. His smell had faded from his unwashed pillow sheet. His clothes hung in a neat row the closet. When would he come home and wear them?

Now, her son was gone too. She was here alone, without the two people who were her life. Her anchors. Bridget didn't know how she would move forward without them. Yet she felt no pain, just white space in her mind and heart.

Unable to focus, Bridget felt a sudden need to make a list of chores. She went to the cupboard to get a pencil and pad. When she returned and started to write, she had to stop. She couldn't write, because the pad was suddenly wet, and her hand was shaking. The pad and pencil dropped from her hand as she slid to the floor, her body trembling.

Chapter Nine

TIM HELD HIS AUNT'S DIRECTIONS to St. Jude's in his jacket pocket as he walked the two blocks from their apartment to the subway. He descended the dank, urine-scented stairway to catch the E train to Woodhaven. Dozens of people stood on the subway platform, many feigning invisibility behind their vertically folded newspapers as they awaited their train. When it arrived, the crowd formed four power wedges and surged toward the open doors, buffeting Tim to the back of the second wedge. A silent, unsmiling Samaritan held the sliding door open for Tim to squeeze through.

Fifteen minutes later, older and wiser, Tim braced himself for a second crush when the train reached his station and the door slid open. He followed the departing passengers to the exit and surfaced to the sounds of heavy traffic, honking horns, and shouting people. Tim stopped at a newsstand and questioned the thin attendant there, who had a deeply lined, jaundiced face, wearing a greasy, gray woolen cap. The attendant removed the cigarette dangling from his lips, proffered a phlegmy cough, then pointed Tim down the street and to the right.

After a five-minute walk, Tim arrived at his new school. He passed a tall, marble statue of a robed figure holding a Bible in his left hand, his opened right hand and his eyes elevated toward the sky. The inscription on the heavy brass plaque read "St. Jude's High School."

Tim entered a large, marble-floored vestibule with a wide glass case filled with trophies, religious statuary, and photos of school administrators. The centerpiece of the glass case was an artist's reverential image of a blissful St. Jude with the subscript: "Patron Saint of Lost Souls." The main hallway reverberated with the clatter and chatter of students moving rapidly in all directions. Tim was feeling numbingly suspended in a cyclorama when a gray-haired cleric in a black robe, sensing the boy's disorientation, approached him.

Tim showed him the class schedule and room assignments that had been mailed to Mrs. Mary Laherty, and the cleric directed him down the hallway and to the left. Tim thanked him, then waded into the crowded hallway. Two minutes later, he found his designated homeroom, where students clustered outside, waiting for the door to be unlocked.

Three students wearing varsity letter jackets stood near the doorsill like barroom bouncers guarding access to the classroom. John Cooper, a tall, thick-necked, broad-shouldered athlete smirked when he saw Tim walk down the hall. He elbowed his fellow football player, Jeff Benson, a 250-pound behemoth with shaggy blond hair and a dull putty face. He then alerted Tyrone Blake, a tall lean black student with a sensitive face, sharp, untrusting cat eyes, and a sullen manner. Blake sported a winged foot on his jacket, signifying his varsity letter for track and field.

Cooper gestured with his head as he spoke. "Look what just popped out of the clown car."

Benson and Blake laughed at the sight of Tim in his baggy woolen pants and his heavy, slightly torn blue sweater. Cooper grabbed Benson's arm and winked at their friend. "Come with me. Play time!"

The trio approached Tim. "Hey friend!" Cooper said. "What

the fuck planet are you from?" Caught off guard, Tim was unsure whether this was a friendly or hostile greeting.

Choosing to think friendly, Tim said, "Planet Ireland, County Sligo. Tim Connolly's me name." He extended his hand. Cooper kept his hands on his hips and ignored the gesture. Tim dropped his hand and looked around uncomfortably at the disinterested student onlookers.

"So, this is what a real-life Irishman looks like!" said Cooper, turning to Blake and Benson. "I *heard* they were dirty and smelled like shit, but I never expected this!" Cooper waved his hand in front of his face as if to dispel a foul odor. Tim shuffled his feet nervously. Blake laughed but also tried to pull Cooper away. "And look at these clothes!" Cooper said, as he threw off Blake's arm and grabbed Tim's homemade sweater. "Your drunken mother knit this?"

Tim swiped Cooper's hand. "Keep yer bloody hands off me."

"I'll keep my hands off you, ass swipe," said Cooper, giving Tim a violent shove, knocking him off his feet. "How's that for hands off, donkey?"

Tim stood up slowly, nervously brushing the dust off his pants. He looked away from Cooper, confused and frightened. Cooper started toward him again, but Blake intervened and pulled Cooper back just as Father Kenney, the school principal, turned the corner and noticed Tim bent over, still dusting his trousers. The priest, a tall man with wavy gray hair and a placid, imperturbable manner, recognized the athletes.

"Blake. Mr. Benson. Mr. Cooper," he said. "What's all the fuss, here?"

"Nothing, Father. Just goofin'," said Blake. The priest looked suspiciously at all parties. Then he turned to Tim.

"And who are you, young man? You're new around here."

Tim answered, his voice shaking. "Tim Connolly, Father."

The priest replied, "An Irish accent? Where from?

"County Sligo, Father. Fishing village called Mullaghmore." Tim glared at Cooper, who stood behind the priest's back, mouthing an obscenity and shaking his hand with the universal jerkoff gesture.

Father Kenney continued, "I visited Sligo many years ago. Beautiful place. My parents are from Galway."

"Yes sir," Tim answered disinterestedly.

"Well, good luck to you, son. I hope you prosper at St. Jude's."

"Thank you, Father," said Tim.

As Father Kenney walked away, he regarded Cooper suspiciously. When the priest turned a corner in the hallway, Cooper pointed menacingly at Tim and waved a fist before entering the classroom. Blake tried to pull Cooper away, but he angrily threw off his friend's arm before relenting. Tim waited until his tormentors were seated inside the classroom before he ventured in and took his seat.

###

After leaving an hour-long orientation from his homeroom teacher, Brother Richard Powell, Tim avoided Cooper, Benson, and Blake and followed a separate group of classmates to the bookstore. He collected his bag of assigned books, then waded through the crowded hallway till he found his locker. Passing students jostled Tim, causing his books to fall from the bag. After gathering them up and stacking them in his locker, Tim checked his schedule and headed for his next destination—the locker room for gym equipment.

There, Tim took his place at the back of another line. His head felt like it was filled with buzzing bees. He wondered if this day would ever end.

A student helper, a short chubby sophomore named Charlie Driscoll, was handing out gym equipment in mesh nylon sacks. Hidden from Tim, Cooper and his two friends snuck into the back of the equipment cage. Cooper called Driscoll aside.

"Hey, Fat Ass! See that strange looking bird over there?" He pointed at Tim. Driscoll spied Tim and nodded. "I want you to give him this equipment sack. "Got it?" Cooper handed him a sack with a torn shirt, small, worn shorts, a jock, and two different-sized sneakers.

"Sure, Coop, whatever you say."

Shortly after Cooper, Benson, and Blake left the cage, Tim picked up his equipment bag and put it in his locker. He never checked the contents.

Chapter Ten

TERENCE'S FACE WAS BRUISED AND SWOLLEN, and his ribs still ached from the beating that had been administered by two guards in the corner of the empty cafeteria before he had even taken residence in his cell. His maiden trip to his cell had featured a shuffling promenade past a receiving line of fellow prisoners, more like phantoms, or the motionless, blanched inhabitants of Homer's underworld.

It took Terence several weeks in H-Block before the full measure of desolation seeped into his consciousness. He was now a resident of a world he knew existed in the annals of human darkness, but to be *himself* completely trapped in this world, this world of steel, concrete, and barbed wire, assaulted his senses, plummeting him into a despair so deep he wasn't sure he would be able to climb out. The daily sight of emaciated, unwashed men wrapped in blankets, the rank smells of their body odor and excrement, the sounds of their groaning from daily beatings by sadistic guards, the taste of rotten, infested food, the feeling of violent fists and batons assailing his body—all of this introduced him to a universe of pain a body might unhappily learn to endure. But the absence of Bridget and Tim, and the loss of their simple, predictable life, inflicted pain that seemed beyond enduring. It awakened him to the naked fragility of the world he'd taken for granted. The unimaginable had become real.

Chapter Eleven

WHILE TIM FINISHED DRYING THE POTS, pans, and dishes, Gary sipped tea and read the evening paper. Mary watched Peter Jennings on the evening news. As Tim placed the last of the dishes in the cupboard, Mary called him.

"Why don't ye come and join us, Tim?"

"Yes ma'am." He walked over and sat in the empty rocker.

Mary asked, "How was your first day, lad?"

"Fine, I guess. Confusing some," Tim replied.

"First day's always the toughest," she said cheerfully. "You'll adjust in no time."

Tim nodded absentmindedly. Gary glanced up from his newspaper for a moment, tempted to add something to the strained conversation. He thought better of it and resumed reading. After a brief, leaden silence, Tim stood and stretched.

"I've some work for tomorrow, so I'll be sayin good night to ye." Mary rose to embrace him, but he instinctively took a step backward.

"Yes, then. Well, good night, Tim," she said, embarrassed.

As Tim awkwardly retreated to his room, Mary looked at Gary, raised her brows, and shrugged her shoulders. Gary shook his head as if to say *Why do you even bother?* and returned to his newspaper.

"Oh, Tim. One more thing," Mary called after him with a strained expression. "I went to Sears today and bought ye some shirts, slacks, and underwear. Ye should be good now, for a while."

Tim forced a smile. "Thank ye, ma'am."

Hidden behind his paper, Gary pursed his lips and shook his head as Tim disappeared into his room.

"Marty's room," he muttered to himself.

Tim unpacked his books and placed them on his small desk. He opened one and tried to read but quickly closed it, frustrated. Heading to the bathroom, he used the toilet, took a shower, brushed his teeth, and worried a pimple on the side of his cheek. Before climbing into bed, he picked up the photo of his dead cousin, touched the Purple Heart and the Silver Star, then carefully replaced it.

He flicked off the light switch and settled into his cousin's bed. Gazing at the ceiling, Tim conjured a home movie of the perfect day back home when he and Millie were herding sheep on the grassy hillside behind their home.

Standing in place, he made a slow turn, relishing the isolation, the mute companionship of the rocky hills around him and the dark cloudy sky above. Suddenly, he took off running, running at full speed across a rocky meadow. While Millie paced him, he ran down a quiet country road, a tunnel of tall hedgerows speckled with pink and purple patches of red clover. Neighbors smiled and waved and shouted, "Hey Timmy!" as he passed them. When he came to a stop some distance from his home, a broad smile creased his face. He saw a gauzy image of his father and mother waving to him.

His fantasy dissolved, and Tim's eyes glistened though his smile. His buzzing brain made it difficult to find sleep.

Chapter Twelve

WITH TERENCE AND TIM GONE, Bridget had trouble sleeping as well. She had no appetite, just nibbling, mouselike, at scraps of bread and cheese. She sipped the infrequent glass of water or cup of tea when her mouth was dry. Intermittently, she wept, but for the most part, she managed one chore after the other in stoic, even robotic, fashion, hoping that simple movement might chase away anxious thoughts and feelings.

When she went to market, neighbors reacted differently to her. Mrs. Boyle avoided extended conversation, anxious to seem concerned without expending the necessary time or energy. Kitty Lenehan was actually concerned, but she avoided discussing Bridget's problems, shy about scratching a still-unhealed wound. Betsy Swanson avoided Bridget altogether, pretending she didn't notice her.

That was fine. Bridget herself had not yet crafted the words to define the depths of what she was feeling, never mind responding with anything more than a "Fine, thanks!" when Mrs. Phelan politely asked, "How are ye?" in the butcher shop queue.

Strangely, few neighbors asked about Terence. Some gossipy types, like the Flanagan sisters, even speculated that maybe he had, in fact, been a terrorist all this time. He did, after all, show a nasty temper on the pitch when he was a younger lad. And sure, wasn't his grandfather himself a notorious and violent rebel?

The melodrama was exhausting. Bridget just wanted to stay

home and sit in front of the fire and talk to Millie. Nothing else. But wouldn't she be needing money to survive, if only to pay the phone bill in the expectation of news about her "boys," if only to afford petrol for the car trip to Maze to see Terence?

Help came from Dermot Casey, the fishmonger. He graciously offered Bridget part-time work during one of her visits to his market, and she accepted. Perhaps, she thought, being out of the house a few hours every day would be a good thing.

At Casey's market, Bridget managed her work in efficient silence. Her cheerful personality and her usual concern for the health and well-being of others had vanished. Casey's shop was mercifully busy from opening to closing, except for the odd day when all the fresh fish on ice in his window sold out before five. Bridget now spent her afternoons wrapping fish and seafood as well as working the cash register. By the end of her workday, she was always weary. The dark spirits who visited her nightly, however, were unconcerned with her fatigue.

During her second week at Casey's, Maeve Grogan, a childhood friend from Tubbercurry, came into the shop and was startled to see her. Maeve had been on holiday abroad with her husband, Joe, and hadn't seen Bridget in months nor heard about her situation.

"Bridget, me love," she said, "I didn't expect to see ye here. I'd ask how ye are, but ye look like hell. Are ye sick? I hope to God no!"

Bridget offered Maeve a short and unsweet summary of her recent setbacks.

"Well, this is feckin unacceptable," Maeve said. "Ye and I have got to talk. What time do ye get out of here? I'll be getting us a bottle of Paddy's, and we'll have us a serious pow-wow."

"Oh Maeve, no," Bridget said. "I'm too worn out to deal with all this now."

"Bullshit," said Maeve. "We're going to dig into this mess for a short while. Tell Casey you're leaving. It's almost closing time anyway."

Maeve was a short, fiercely intelligent woman with sharp blue eyes that sparkled with laughter one moment and bristled with anger the next. Her energy radiated through every atom in her body and put a charge in anyone within ten feet of her. A prominent figure in the Sligo real estate market, she had a blunt, outspoken manner and a gift for demanding and getting her way. Despite having four small children, Maeve and her husband, Joe (a prominent figure in the Gaelic Athletic Association and an All-Ireland Right Corner Back in Gaelic Football twenty years earlier), ran a successful B&B during high season, so successful that she was able to send overflow to other, smaller B&Bs in the area, eventually creating a profitable, informal consortium in Tubbercurry. She had an enormous talent for impromptu, irreverent comedy, and a quick-talking skill at arranging events for neighbors, as well as tourists, before they even knew their other plans had been scuttled. Maeve ultimately delighted those under her spell, because she would, pied-piper-like, lead her boarders to unique, out-of-the way pubs, restaurants, special events, and ancient ruins. She saw to it that local pubs got their share of the tourists' cash. She was, in the eyes of her neighbors, the unofficial mayor of Tubbercurry. As such, she was loved. But she was also unloved: some local pub owners, grudgingly beholden to her, felt obliged to open their doors after legal closing hours if Maeve wanted a late drink. She would shout and pound the door until she was admitted. Once inside, she would unleash a torrent of abuse on the reluctant owner, though it usually subsided after her second drink.

Back at Bridget's cottage, Maeve pulled two glasses from the cupboard and sat at the kitchen table with Bridget, filling them with whisky. She drank hers straight; Bridget placed a separate glass of water on the table to dilute hers.

Then Maeve asked her for the full story, top to bottom. Millie jumped on Bridget's lap as she began. She concentrated on petting Millie, avoiding eye contact with Maeve as she spoke.

When she finished her story, Maeve started carving at Bridget's pain like an Easter ham.

"First of all," she said, then paused. "Bridget, love, look at me please." Bridget turned and lifted her head. "Both of yer men are still living. They're not dead and buried. Sure, and they may be in for some tough times, where they are away from ye and everything they love. And this is no bed of roses for ye. I get that. But shit, Bridget, this is life. Everybody hits some rough patches along the way, some worse than others, sure, but that's the deal. I've had two late-term miscarriages. Broke me bloody heart. Twice! And doesn't me own son have a poster of a sad-eyed beagle on his bedroom wall that says, 'Life's a bitch and then ye die'? That's me boy, Padraig, and he's only eleven year's old for Christ's sake!"

Bridget laughed for the first time in weeks and took a gentle sip of her drink.

"But yer men are still alive," Maeve continued. "So, there's hope. We Irish are experts with the darkness and despair. And don't we women specialize in it? Like me dear late mother, God rest her soul! She was never more alive than when some neighbor's death or pitiful event activated her tear ducts. Oh, the wailing and the feckin keening! It's bloody contagious. And eventually we pass it on to our men, who plainly could give less of a shite. All they want to do is mount us and drink their porter, and not necessarily in that order."

Bridget took a second sip and laughed even more. Maeve emptied her glass in one gulp and poured another.

"And don't get me started on the Church and all this 'God's will' bullshit. Or . . . God is testing us. That's it, *testing us*. Sure, and what the feck happens if we fail this test? If we give in to pain and grief? Do we go to hell? And don't get me started on hell . . ."

"Ye'r right, Maeve." Bridget raised her hand to slow the woman's surging momentum. "Yes. Ye'r *absolutely* right! I must take control of my sadness."

"Of course, love," said Maeve. "Ye'r a strong beautiful woman, but ye look like a car wreck right now. Ye've lost weight. Ye've got bloody bags under your eyes. Seems like ye've even lost the will to live. But this is a new day for women. We women are learning to take control and not just collapse on our goddamn fainting beds every time we get a whiff of sorrow. We must cease being paralyzed by problems created by stupid men."

Bridget nodded her head in approval and thanked her friend profusely. "Ye have any food in this house?" Maeve asked. "Let's finish this bottle and have something to eat. I'm feckin starving."

Chapter Thirteen

THE LOCKER ROOM BUSTLED WITH STUDENTS scrambling to change for gym class. Locker doors slammed and boys jostled one another, cursing, pushing, and laughing as they crowded out.

Tim lagged behind, struggling to put on his jock, socks, shirt, and shorts. They were all too small, too tight, and made him look ridiculous. He struggled with his sneakers—one was too small; the other was too big and had no laces. When the bell rang, he headed for the gym, carrying his sneakers. When he arrived late, a student near the entrance directed him to the back of the line. Cooper, Benson, and Blake relished the sight of him in his odd clothes and alerted others to the prank.

Gym Teacher, John Quigley, a trim ruddy-faced man of medium height, with thinning salt-and-pepper hair combed straight back, walked to the front of the gym with a noticeable limp. He wore a dark blue running suit with a whistle around his neck. He blew it twice to silence the students' chatter. Then he organized them into four columns, ten students per column.

"Gentleman, I am Mr. Quigley. This is my first term at St. Jude's, and though I'm sorry to hear that your previous instructor had a heart attack and will miss the remainder of the school year, I am nonetheless pleased to be here working with such fine young men."

At the back of one column, Cooper whispered to Blake, "What bullshit."

"We only have a fifty-minute class to do our work, and I have a full lineup of calisthenics for you," Quigley continued, "so let's get right to it. I'll explain things as we go along. First, we'll warm up with a set of twenty-five jumping jacks. Let's begin." He started counting, and the students executed their jumping jacks with varying levels of skill and coordination.

Meanwhile, Brother Frank Russell, a tall, rangy man wearing a long, black robe and clutching a rosary in his left hand, entered the gym and proceeded to weave slowly among the jumping students. His lordly manner suggested ownership of this space and its inhabitants. He sported a wry, sardonic grin as he watched the flailing ineptitude of the more hopelessly clumsy boys. He stopped next to Cooper and playfully punched him in the shoulder while the exercises continued. Smiling, Cooper responded by assuming a boxer's stance.

"How's my best linebacker and shot putter?" Brother Frank said.

"Great, Brother! Good to be back," said Cooper, relishing the attention.

Brother Frank laughed and patted his shoulder. Next, he walked to a thin, red-haired, freckle-faced student and playfully smacked him on the back of the head.

The student responded with a nervous laugh. "Hi, Brother! How are you?"

"Doing great, tough guy. Stay outta trouble this semester."

"You bet, Brother." Frank wandered over to the side of the gym and observed the class. Quigley ignored the brother's distracting engagements and moved on to the next exercise.

"Okay, gentlemen. Let's go immediately into our squat thrusts."

While the teacher demonstrated the squat thrust, Tim tried to adjust his tight shorts. When the exercise began, the agile students executed it flawlessly. The overweight and ill-coordinated grunted and flopped on their bellies like beached seals. One student ripped a loud fart, causing those around him to dissolve into gales of laughter. As Tim squatted, the back of his shorts ripped up the seam, partially exposing his butt and the straps of his jock.

"Bloody shite!" Tim struggled to cover his partially exposed butt. The student next to him noticed Tim's dilemma and laughed, pointing it out to the boy next to him. Quigley noticed the disturbance and brought the exercise to a halt.

". . . And, stop! All right, gentlemen. At ease. Let's take a breather. I see Brother Frank, our athletic director and football coach, has joined us. Brother Frank, would you like to offer a few words to our senior class?"

The cleric placed his rosary in his pocket and strutted to the front of the gym.

"Thank you, Mr. Quigley. Welcome back, seniors! This is a big semester for you—your final term before we send you into the world. I want you to make the most of your final days here. As you all know, St. Jude is the patron saint of lost souls. I hope during your time here, he has helped you find your souls and that he has given you a good foundation for life. But life can wear you down, and we can all lose ourselves from time to time, so always remember St. Jude, and what you learned here."

He paused to take a deep breath. "Be kind to yourself and to all those who may need your help. You can do this. After all, as seniors, you are the pride of St. Jude's!"

The students cheered his words. Brother Frank raised his hand to stop the cheering. He turned toward Mr. Quigley. "Now, briefly, let me tell you something about your new gym instructor," he said. "Thirty some odd years ago, Mr. Quigley was one of the finest sprinters and middle-distance runners in the world, earning him a spot on the US Olympic team. Unfortunately for him, the Korean War intervened, and a severe leg wound ended Marine Captain Quigley's military career as well as his running career. But we are lucky to have him at St. Jude's and wish him only the greatest success." Quigley shuffled uncomfortably and looked down at his feet. "By the way, any runners out there should know that Mr. Quigley will be the new coach of our track team."

Cooper, Benson, and Blake noticed the dire condition of Tim's shorts and alerted more students to the developing prank. Tim's predicament generated increasingly noisy and scornful laughter. Brother Frank strained impatiently to see what was happening.

"What's going on back there?" he shouted.

Cooper shouted back amid laughter, while pointing at Tim, "Looks like a case of indecent exposure, Brother!"

Frank called to Tim. "You back there, come up here."

Tim looked around, nervous and confused.

Cooper whispered to him. "He means you, douchebag." He turned to Benson and Blake. "Jesus, this is perfect!" Tim shuffled to the front of the gym with the back of his shorts flapping, holding both sneakers in his right hand.

As the laughter continued, Brother Frank shouted, "Silence!" The class went silent. Frank squinted at Tim, as he shuffled forward in his sweat socks. "I don't know you. You must be new here."

"Yes, sir."

"That's 'Yes, *Brother*,' young man."

Tim fidgeted. "Yes, sir. Uh, yes, Brother." Nervously, he raised himself up and down on his toes.

"Stop moving," said Brother Frank menacingly.

"Yes, sir, uh, Brother." Tim heard students chuckling and turned round, looking nervously back at them.

"Look at me, young man, not them. Where did you get this foolish outfit?"

"This is what the lad handed me, Brother," said Tim.

"What's your name?" Brother Frank asked.

"Tim Connolly." Tim continued to bob up and down on his toes.

"I told you to stop your damn fidgeting when I speak to you."

"Yes, Brother." Tim grimaced nervously. Brother Frank mistook his expression for a grin.

"You think this is funny? You think this is a joke?"

Tim's voice cracked. "No, sir. No . . . Brother." He grimaced and bobbed again.

Suddenly, Brother Frank snapped. He viciously smacked Tim in the face, forcing him to stagger back. Tim yelped in pain. The brother stepped toward him and smacked him full force with his other hand. Tim spun around, slipped, and fell to one knee.

"Do you think I'm here to amuse you, Mr. *Donnelly*?" he asked. Stunned, Tim shook his head and put his hand to his bleeding lip. "Speak up. Do you?" he repeated, as spittle formed in the corners of his mouth and his eyes reddened.

"No, Brother," Tim murmured through his swollen, bleeding mouth.

"Stand up. I can't hear you. Stand up!"

Tim stood, hunched over, experiencing shock and shame in equal measure. As if excited by the sight of his wounded prey, Brother Frank struck again before Tim could fully straighten up, this time smacking Tim's left cheek with his right hand, spinning him sideways. Mr. Quigley took a halting step forward, not sure what to do. Tim's eyes welled with tears as he held his bleeding mouth. The gym became graveyard silent.

Brother Frank broke the silence and sneered, "You. Get out of my sight."

The shaken boy gathered himself, then staggered past the grinning trio of Cooper, Benson, and Blake. Brother Frank, shaking with rage, glanced at Mr. Quigley, gesturing for him to resume class. Then he retreated from the gym in a dark and angry mood. Quigley intercepted Tim before he exited the gym. He gently placed his hand on Tim's shoulder to assess his condition. Tim pulled away as though jolted by electric current.

"Mr. Connolly, go to the shower and get cleaned up," Quigley said. "Be sure to get yourself some decent equipment before next class." Tim strained to disguise his pain and humiliation. Cooper, Benson, and Blake smacked hands as Tim left the gym with ripped shorts, sneakers in hand, and blood on his mouth, hands, and his shirt.

Quigley then turned to the class. "All right, everyone. Settle down. Spread out for a set of push-ups . . ."

Chapter Fourteen

BRIDGET UNEXPECTEDLY RECEIVED her first pass to see Terence eight weeks after his arrest. The usual three-hour drive to Belfast took more than five this time, due to the numerous Royal Ulster Constabulary and British Army checkpoints. When she arrived at "Her Majesty's Prison Maze," a British soldier escorted her to "H-Block"—a separate prison within a prison designed specifically to house paramilitary and political prisoners.

Terence's assault on the soldiers attacking his grandfather had earned him the status of a political prisoner. The facility itself was harsh and forbidding. In addition to fifteen-foot fences, an eighteen-foot concrete wall topped with razor wire encompassed each block; all gates on the complex were made of solid steel and electronically operated. Each square plot encased a housing compound shaped like a giant H.

A grim-visaged, overweight prison guard in a gunmetal-gray uniform escorted Bridget to a room with a long, wide table and a heavy, wire fence, separating the prisoner from his visitor. Bridget sat for twenty anxious minutes awaiting Terence. Accompanied by his own guard, he shuffled barefoot in ankle chains into the visiting area, wrapped in a stained gray blanket. His hair was greasy and unkempt. A patchy black-and-gray beard darkened his face. His eyes were swollen and colored with bruises, and his nose had clearly been broken. His muscular body had diminished from foul and insufficient rations, not to mention lack of fresh air and exercise.

Bridget shrieked at the sight of him. Terence agonized over her response and labored to calm her. He whispered to her how much he loved her, how much he missed her and Tim. He spoke ever more softly to Bridget until she caught her breath.

After a few gasping minutes, she was able to listen to him. Terence asked how Tim was doing. Haltingly, Bridget mentioned that Tim had recently started classes in a parochial school in New York City, but she had no recent news. She explained why she thought Tim would be safer with his aunt and uncle for now. Terence shook his head with grim acceptance. He asked how she was faring with the farm and her job. She just shrugged her shoulders and wiped her nose. Then she told Terence about her job at Casey's Market and the good counsel and support she'd received from Maeve.

Terence considered downplaying the abuse he and others were receiving at the hands of the guards, but he decided that Bridget should know what was going on, so she could share it with the outside world. When her weeping subsided, Terence chronicled the beatings. The soldier he had punched in Belcoo had made a special visit to H-Block to administer his first in-house beating. That one broke his nose. He told her that the punishments consisted of physical abuse as well as water, food, and sleep deprivation. Terence mentioned that many prisoners like him were now "on the blanket" because they refused to wear prison uniforms and be treated like criminals, insisting instead that they were prisoners of war. Some of the prisoners, in desperation, had begun hunger strikes, though he was not tempted in that direction.

Bridget asked, "Do ye know how long they will keep ye? When might they let ye go? Don't they know ye'r not IRA?"

Terence shrugged and shook his head. "No, love, I have no idea how long they plan to keep me. As for not being IRA . . . at this point, they don't care."

"What happened to your grandfather?" Bridget inquired.

"I don't know whether he had a heart attack or just collapsed from exhaustion. But they released him, for medical reasons I assume. I've heard nothing."

"Maybe they didn't want the publicity of a famous old man dying on their watch," Bridget suggested.

"Or maybe they figured he was too old to be a threat," said Terence. "I don't know."

They were permitted five more minutes together. Bridget told him about the painful changes in Mullaghmore and her odd relations with their neighbors. She also mentioned that she was maintaining the farm, but it lacked the attention to detail and the love that he and Tim had lavished on it day in and day out.

Bridget thought but could not say, *Like you both did for me. Day in and day out.*

Then the guard ended their meeting. Bridget said she would return as soon as possible. They touched their hands on the grate and separated.

Chapter Fifteen

MARY HAD JUST DROPPED A TEASPOON of salt into a pot of boiling water when Tim came through the door. She wiped her hands on her apron and turned to greet him. Tim, though, darted quickly into his room and shut the door. Curious, Mary approached his bedroom and knocked.

"Tim, lad. Are ye all right?"

Yes, ma'am. Just tired," he murmured through his swollen lip.

Tim went to the bathroom and splashed cold water on his damaged face. He moistened a face cloth and pressed it lightly against his bruises.

Mary returned to the stove but kept glancing back at the door to Tim's room, worried. While she added peeled and cubed potatoes to the boiling water, Gary arrived, hung his coat in the closet, and greeted her with a kiss.

Noticing her agitation, he asked, "Something wrong?"

Mary gestured with her head to Tim's room. "It's Tim. He just bolted to his room and shut the door. He sounded kinda funny."

Gary said, "Oh, for Christ's sake, Mary. He's a teenager! There's always something."

At that, Tim came out of his room. He stood before them, head down, sullen and tentative. Mary and Gary went silent when they saw Tim's cut, swollen lips, eyes, and bruised cheeks.

"Dear God in heaven," Mary said, "Timmy, what happened to ye?"

Gary bristled and clenched his fists. "Did those punks around the corner do this?"

Tim shook his head. "No. Some teacher named 'Brother Frank.'"

Gary erupted, "A brother! What did you do wrong?"

Tim shrugged his shoulders and shook his head.

Mary said, "Tim, now, this is a man of God. He wouldn't just be hittin' ye for just no reason."

Tim replied curtly, "Maybe God told him to do it."

"Don't get fresh with your aunt, young man," growled Gary.

"I'm sorry, sir. I'm just tired like."

Mary moved toward Tim to comfort him, but the boy pulled away and put his hands up. She froze, unsure what to do. Then she regrouped, wiping her hands on her apron.

"Okay, let's eat then," she said.

They solemnly took their places at the table, lowering their heads as Gary spoke. "Bless us O Lord and these, thy gifts . . ."

Back in his room after barely touching his dinner, Tim leaned over his bathroom sink and splashed more cold water on his face. He again checked his bruises in the mirror. Then he stared into the mirror and projected himself into a Sligo bog with his father.

He and Terence were slicing blocks of spongy turf and setting them gingerly on the bank. Ben Bulben stared disinterestedly as, dirty and sweating, they finished slicing the fragrant, moist peat and stacked it onto the back of the cart. Once loaded, Terence gathered and snapped the reins, and Zeus pulled the wagon slowly among pink rosemary blossoms as the sun set across the bog. Then Terence handed the reins to Tim and put his arm over his son's shoulder as they rode away.

When the image in the mirror dissolved, Tim said, "Jaysus, Da. I hate this bloody place. I want to come home."

Chapter Sixteen

CREAKING LIKE A PRIED-OPEN SEPULCHER, the steel gates of Maze Prison squealed grudgingly, releasing a hobbled Brian Connolly. Walking now with the aid of a crutch, Brian made his way to the roadside bus stop near the tall, white guard tower. A drizzling rain fell as he waited for the bus.

After fifteen minutes, the bus arrived and took him the thirteen miles to Belfast. His first stop was White's Tavern. The oldest pub in Belfast had a reliably Catholic clientele, which immediately soothed his nerves. Sidling up to the bar, Brian removed his rain-soaked coat, propped his elbows on the mahogany bar, exchanged pleasantries with the bartender, and placed his order. As he sipped his first Guinness pint, chased by a mellow Black Bush shooter, he moaned softly and raised his eyes to heaven. "Thank ye, Jaysus." After a third round, a mellowing Brian was joined by Mike Scully, one of the mates he had planned to meet in Enniskillen. Scully took a stool next to Brian, shook his hand, and looked somberly at his old friend.

"Been a long while, Connolly," he said.

"It has been a long time indeed, Mr. Scully," said Brian, sporting a cheerful grin.

As he checked out Brian's appearance, Scully's face darkened. "Hate to say it, old friend, but time has been unkind. Ye're not lookin' real good." Brian, now comfortably inebriated, laughed, then blamed his diminished appearance on recent applications of fists, feet, and batons to his face, back, and legs.

"You'd be amazed, Mr. Scully," said Brian, now slurring his words, "how little respect these twats have for the elderly. Not a fuckin' shred. One night, three screws pummeled me like a godamm—ah, whatchamacallit. One of them, ah, Mexican things."

"Piñata?"

"Yeah, that. Three of them bastards, just pounding the piss outta me like they thought toys and candy bars would come flyin' outta me arse."

Scully laughed. "Well, did they?"

"Maybe. I'm not sure." Brian laughed and wheezed. "What did happen though was I had a feckin seizure and collapsed. The seizure apparently touched their black hearts," he said. "The fuckers had their fun and probably calculated no advantage in continuing to feed a beaten-up, broken-down old badger like me, especially if I were to croak on their watch. The saved paperwork alone probably sealed the deal."

Brian paused and drained the rest of his drink and lit a cigarette. "The bastards just made me angrier, then—sorry I didn't kill more of them . . . when I had the chance."

Scully said he was just glad to see him out and alive, though he couldn't help shaking his head and again mentioning Brian's "altered appearance."

"Still with my looks, eh, Mr. feckin Universe?" Brian stood, leaned forward, and wobbled on his crutch, slurring as he spoke. "Lookie here, they knocked out three of me side teeth." Brian staggered as he exposed his gums. "Then they cracked something in me back. The black eyes have healed, but I can hardly stand up, so I'm slouching and hunching like feckin Quasimodo. And maybe . . . what de ye think, maybe . . . this crutch here is also a feckin giveaway." He stood precariously as he held his crutch aloft, took a deep breath, grinned, and coughed. "But, what the bloody hell, I'm still alive. But I most truly, most truly want revenge on these fuckers, Mr. Scully. And also for me grandson and his family."

"Aye! Well, that's good fortune, me friend, because revenge is just what me and Flynn have in mind, not just rehashing the old days," said Scully.

"What are ye on about? asked Brian.

"You, me, and Flynn. Doin' something useful while we still have some blood in our veins. We ain't dead yet, though you look pretty feckin' close."

Scully laughed, and Brian scowled. "Flynn was supposed to be here," Scully continued. "He and I have been communicating over the last year, and we came up with some ideas we wanted to share with ye. I don't know where he is right now. He was supposed to be here. He said he had errands to run." Scully paused and scratched his head. "Knowing him, cheap bastard that he is—and always has been— he probably thought he might have to stand a round or two."

"Aye, indeed. I remember that feature about our Mr. Flynn," said Brian, sporting a drunken grin. "A rare warrior and a funny lad, but Jaysus, a notorious skinflint. I remember old Colonel Leahy once said Flynn was so cheap, he'd save the grease off a fart. But what about these plans?"

"Flynn has some contacts with some of the young fellas in Armagh," said Scully. "They have a small army of snipers, bombers, lads who provide safe houses for guys on the run. Word is they're even coordinating a jailbreak with some of the lads in H-Block. Flynn said they'd be happy to meet us. I'm not sure why, but maybe we can help them. Ye know, like the old days—'Once more into the breach,' said the Lone Ranger."

"Well, me friend, count me in. But first, let's have us another round or two. Then we'll find Flynn and these young fellas," said Brian as he waved to the bartender and shakily readjusted himself on his barstool with the help of his crutch. "Maybe they can also put me on to a good dentist and a chiropractor. And, by the way . . . that wasn't the Lone Ranger, for fuck's sake."

In his younger years, Mike Scully was an accomplished sniper during the war of independence. Prior to any troop movement, he would scout the back roads and hills, looking for information and soft targets. He was slight of build and sported a thatch of tight, curly blond hair. He had a determinedly serious manner; he smiled little and laughed even less. But he moved like a bobcat through the shadowy woods, using his high-powered binoculars to track enemy movements and encampments. He rambled through the hills, seeking giant stones, lofty cliffs, tall trees, or thick brush to establish his position. Then he would camouflage his perch and set himself before zeroing in on his targets—adjusting the telescopic sight on his 1903-model Springfield rifle, his bolt-action "baby" with its five-round internal magazine. In one encounter outside of Limerick in 1919, Scully took out nine Black and Tans, using two separate, prepared sites. He escaped unseen, so effectively was he concealed. Scully loved retelling the tale of that day. His few living friends, like Brian, always enjoyed the retelling, especially when embellishments were added. In one dramatic version, the number of dead Black and Tans exceeded fifteen.

Chapter Seventeen

Tim, cheek and lip still swollen, entered class just as the bell rang. As he took his seat in the back corner of the classroom, the other students glanced at him, a few sympathetically, most unconcerned.

Cooper whispered to Benson and Blake. All three turned to look at him. Tim stared straight ahead, impassive.

After wishing his students a cheerful good morning, reedy-voiced Brother Henry turned his back to the class and began filling the chalkboard with streams of numbers and symbols, feverishly tracking the roots of quadratic equations from their coefficients. Tim lay his head down on his unopened book and fell asleep.

###

The runners entered in the Cliffony-Mullaghmore Road Race assembled at the starting line—the intersection of N16 and the regional Borough Road. The trail consisted of 3.6 kilometers of winding, hilly road, with the finish line at the Piers Head Hotel in Mullaghmore. Dressed in his coveralls and work boots, Tim thought running against friends and neighbors would be fun. He had never been in a road race, so he had no expectations. When the fifty runners were ready, the starter simply waved a handkerchief and shouted, "Go!"

Since Tim knew nothing about pacing, he just followed the leaders, surprised they were moving so slowly. As the runners neared town, the crowds grew larger; bagpipers lined the streets, rallying the runners to their destination. Twenty-five of the original runners were still tightly packed when they caught sight of the finish line some four hundred meters down the road. Tim was the only one to break from the pack. He easily sprinted the rest of the way, finishing some one hundred meters ahead of second place.

That evening, the town celebrated the fair's ending in McGovern's Pub, a century-old, low-ceilinged, heavy-beamed pub that for this one night only featured Seamus Tansey, "The King of the Concert Flute." Seamus was accompanied by Joe Burke on the accordion, Tommy Peoples on fiddle, and John Gaffney on bodhran. The pub was thick with smoke, craic, man sweat, and laughter. In anticipation of the session, fifteen pints of Guinness lined the bar. The slow draughting caused the porter to bubble leisurely, layer by layer, to the brim, where it settled into a two-inch-thick beige foam that overflowed the brim of the glass until tapster Jimmy Owens scraped the foam to create a perfectly flat creamy head.

Burly and mustachioed, Seamus Tansey led his players to the back corner of the pub. While the players settled and tuned their instruments, the crowd went silent, until Tansey fractured the silence and jolted them with his rousing rendition of "Jim Donaghue's Reel." Tansey's fingers danced over his flute stops while fiddle, accordion, and bodhran wove a multicolored tapestry of sound in and out and around his soaring notes.

Without a break, Tansey followed with "The Pigeon at the Gate" and "The Reel at Mullinvat." The pub rocked with foot stomping, hoots, whistles, and hand clapping. Chairs and tables were spread wide to open space for people to dance, and the floor filled quickly. Tim sat with his small trophy on the table, smiling as he watched his mother and father dancing expertly in a circle of friends. Then Bridget gestured Tim onto the dance floor, and Tim joined his parents in the circle of swirling and foot-stomping friends. And they danced.

The bell signaling the end of class startled Tim. He lifted his head, rubbed his face, and remained seated while everyone else, including the teacher, filed out of classroom. He placed his hand on his book and sighed despondently, wondering how long he would be confined in this woeful, joyless place.

Chapter Eighteen

ST. JUDE'S TRACK WAS AN OLD FACILITY—four hundred meters of crushed, packed cinder that made a distinctive crunching sound when runners punctured the surface with their long-spiked racing shoes during track meets.

No such spikes today—only Keds and Chuck Taylor sneakers. As Mr. Quigley's forty students jogged around the track, warming up, Tim jogged by himself at the very back of the pack. Quigley then whistled the class to the starting line.

"Gentlemen, we have an unseasonably warm afternoon, so I thought we would do some racing today. We'll call it a 'conditioning assessment.'" Sorrowful groans greeted the announcement. Quigley smiled as he gestured to Blake. "As you know, we have one of the city's finest middle-distance runners in our class, the track team's captain, Tyrone Blake. Mr. Blake also holds the school's records for the two-hundred, four-hundred, and eight-hundred meters. Quite a feat." Blake raised his right fist triumphantly. "We all know what he can do," said Quigley, "but I want to check on the rest of you, just to see what kind of shape you are in." More moans greeted this second announcement.

Cooper whispered to Benson and Blake, "Keep it real slow, guys. The gimp's just trying to break our balls."

Quigley heard the boy whispering and turned to him.

"Mr. Cooper. You have an opinion? You're supposed to be our top shot putter and javelin thrower. And a linebacker, too. Don't you believe it's important to run for conditioning?" Cooper smirked as he looked at the other students for approbation.

"Not really, Mr. Q. Never have in the past. Ain't hurt me yet."

"Well, you've got a lot to learn," Quigley said. "Including English grammar. And the name is Mr. Quigley, not Mr. Q." He stared down the smirking Cooper then stepped up to the starting line with his stopwatch and clipboard. "Everybody on the starting line. Two rows if necessary. Let's have some fun. One lap around. Let's see what you've all got."

Tim stood in the outside lane, second row.

Cooper whispered to Blake and Benson, "Let's box this Irish punk at the turn and throw a few elbows in his gut."

"Good idea. Maybe his chin, too." Benson laughed.

Jeff Benson had been a fixture on the football team since his freshman year, primarily because of his size. At six foot three and 250 pounds, he dwarfed most high school players. While he was not particularly fast or agile, he easily pushed opponents aside or flattened them when he got his arms around them. He was beloved by his teammates because, in a championship game against powerhouse arch-rival, Pace High School, Benson got knocked out three separate times but kept coming back into the game claiming he "just got his bell rung." Brother Frank awarded him the game ball after that victory for a game-saving tackle at St. Jude's two-yard line. Benson confessed at the time that he didn't know why Brother Frank presented him with the game ball, since he couldn't remember the last two quarters, never mind the last play.

His bell-ringing blows to the head were also diminishing his academic standing. He was failing every one of his classes, except Phys. Ed. He managed to escape expulsion either because he was protected as one of St. Jude's preeminent "lost souls," or more likely because Brother Frank deemed him essential to the football team's success.

###

Cooper and Benson maneuvered to get near Tim on the starting line. Tim looked suspiciously at them and took two steps backward. Quigley gave a quick signal.

"On your mark, set, go." Quigley pressed his stopwatch as the class moved in a sluggish mass toward the first turn. Cooper and Blake looked around for Tim. He, meanwhile, trotted in last place. As the pack moved around the second turn, at the hundred-meter mark, Tim decided to stretch his legs. His demeanor and his tempo changed as he suddenly surged past everyone, claiming the far outside lane as his own and sprinting to the lead.

Cooper yelled, "What's he doing? That bastard! Go after him, Blake."

Blake obediently broke from the pack and chased Tim.

Tim seemed to relax in a higher gear, striding in a strong, relaxed tempo, gobbling up yards. Blake moved with impressive speed, but he could not close the distance. As they turned into the final straightaway, Tim glanced at Blake over his shoulder. Then he saw Quigley holding his stopwatch at the finish line.

"Come on, Connolly. Kick it in!" he shouted.

Tim looked back again at Blake, increased his pace, and stormed across the finish line. Blake followed thirty meters behind.

Quigley was euphoric. "Fifty-three seconds. Holy cow!" The

rest of the pack scrambled raggedly to the finish line, gasping for air, as Quigley called out their times. When all students had crossed the line, he assembled the class. "Okay, gentlemen," he said. "I see most of you have considerable work to do to improve your conditioning. We'll be doing more of this. Walk one lap around the track, then head to the showers."

As Tim started his cooldown, still breathing from his run, Quigley shouted, "Mr. Connolly!" Tim stopped as the smiling teacher approached him. "Young man, you've got some serious talent. You just ran the four hundred in fifty-three seconds from an outside lane wearing basketball sneakers! Do you know what that means?"

Tim shook his head. "No, sir, I don't."

Quigley smiled and grabbed his shoulder. Tim pulled away as if threatened. Quigley proceeded, nonplussed. "It means you have a remarkable gift. Have you ever raced before?"

"Once," Tim said. "I did a road race at the Sligo Fair last summer."

"And how did you do?" asked Quigley.

Tim raised his eyebrows. "Well, I won, but—"

Quigley interrupted. "Well, son, I want you on my track team. Interested?"

"Track team?" Surprised and bemused, Tim paused. He looked at Quigley and scratched his head. Then he fixed a long, bitter stare at the other students, joking and clowning as they circled the track. He turned to Quigley and spoke with a cold glare and a bitter edge to his voice. "Sure, and why not?"

"Great. We start tomorrow," said Quigley. "Stop by my office later for the team uniform and sweatsuit." He took a pad from his briefcase and wrote on a scrap of paper. "First thing, get yourself downtown to Randy's Sporting Goods today for some proper running shoes—one pair for training and one for racing. Here are the directions." He handed Tim the paper.

"Mr. Quigley, sir, I can't afford—"

"No problem. Tell, Randy, the store manager, that I sent you. He's an old friend. He'll get the shoes you need and put it on my tab."

On the far side of the track, Cooper, Benson, and Blake walked slowly, watching the conversation occurring between Tim and the teacher.

Cooper taunted Blake. "Are you shitting me, Blake?"

Blake reacted dismissively. "Sheeit! This was just one day. A fluke."

"Yeah. Just a one-day fluke," said Cooper.

Chapter Nineteen

BRIAN AND SCULLY ENTERED A GRAY-STONE rowhouse on Enniskillen's "Gallagh Shore Road," one block from Beatty's Chip Shop in a traditionally Catholic neighborhood. They received a hearty welcome from six young fighters, lads between twenty and forty years of age. This crop of rebels—members of the Provisional IRA—had been radicalized by the Bloody Sunday killings in 1972, when British Army paratroopers indiscriminately fired their rifles into hundreds of peaceful, unarmed civilians, wounding twenty-six and killing fourteen, shooting them as they were fleeing or trying to aid the wounded.

Brian had read about the situation in Derry seven years earlier. Shane Doherty, one of the young rebels at the time, remembered how the community reacted. "Factories, shops, stores, banks, and offices all closed in protest, and the streets were deserted. Teachers went on strike, and schools closed."

The anger never subsided. It metastasized.

The future bishop of Derry, Edward Daly, published an open letter in *The Derry Journal* in which he accused "the Colonel of the Parachute Regiment of willful murder . . . of being an accessory before the fact . . . of shooting indiscriminately into a fleeing crowd, of gloating over casualties, of preventing medical and spiritual aid reaching some of the dying." He called these soldiers trained criminals, differing "from terrorists only in the veneer of respectability that a uniform gives them."

Brian and Scully thought they themselves were remarkable for their visceral contempt for the British, but they were gentle midwives compared to their young hosts. One young Provo, a lad named Barry, greeted them with hearty handshakes and words of gratitude for their long sacrifices for Irish independence. Barry had a shaved head, a weightlifter's body, and a tattoo on his neck of a fist holding a lightning bolt. He mentioned that he had been present at the bloody march in Derry. It "transformed him," he said, "into an avenger."

Brian produced a mental snapshot of young Barry as a Hollywood action hero, an Irish Rambo of some sort, posing in front of his mirror holding an AK-47, wearing a tank-top shirt, a red bandana, and a surly expression. Barry explained to Brian and Scully how the strategies and tactics the Provos were employing today were different from in the old days in one very elemental way. In the war of independence, the IRA used conventional weapons like rifles, machine guns, mortars, dynamite, and grenades to wage war against a visible enemy army. Barry said the default weapon of the Provisional IRA, on the other hand, was the car or truck bomb—clocks and electronic circuitry attached to twenty or more sticks of gelignite placed inside a car or truck. "More bang for the buck," he said. He said he felt bad that most of the victims were civilians rather than combatants. He called them unfortunate collateral damage, or "unsuspecting martyrs to the ideal of a united Ireland."

Most citizens of the Irish Republic sympathized with the goals of the Provisional IRA but were appalled by their methods. Critics argued that since the car bomb was detonated from afar, the killings diluted responsibility and took on the detachment of the passive voice. The bomber's physical distance from the horror made killing people more abstract, like dropping a bomb from fifty thousand feet—no messy firefights where the bombers faced death or maiming, or where they might see in real time the twisted faces and the mangled bodies of their victims. In this kind of war, large numbers of people could be obliterated in a single explosion without the bomber ever seeing or being seen by an enemy soldier.

The cold-blooded clarity of Barry's explanation disturbed Brian, making him wonder if the Provos' cause was the same cause he had sworn allegiance to all those years ago. Had the righteous crusade of Easter 1916 finally run its course? Were these lads the "rough beasts" Yeats prophesied? Brian's mind wandered while Barry was still talking. He could not imagine Padraig Pearse endorsing the use of innocent Irish civilians as props in an ongoing campaign of terror.

Barry's glib final comments about how effectively these devices shattered a building or shredded a human body shook Brian from his dark musings.

"Here one minute," said the young man whimsically, "gone the next. Kaboom! Splatto!"

When they were alone, Brian took a deep breath and shook his head in shocked disbelief.

Scully whispered, "Jaysus H. Christ. These lads are serious."

"Maybe fuckin crazy, too," said Brian, sobered by Barry's narrative. He told Scully that once they finished with their business with the planned jailbreak, he would be done.

Chapter Twenty

IN THE ATHLETIC SHOE SECTION of Randy's Sporting Goods, Tim marveled at the variety of running shoes displayed on the shelves. He picked up dozens of different pairs, bouncing some in his hand, amazed at how light they were.

The store clerk approached and asked Tim what he was looking for.

Tim said he wasn't sure. "Those, I guess." He pointed to an entire section of training and competition shoes on the shelf and selected twenty-five different boxes. The clerk grumbled under his breath as he stacked them all next to Tim's chair and footstool.

Tim spent more than an hour deliberating. The clerk, the lone one on duty, worked with other customers and glanced over intermittently as Tim casually opened one box after another. He tried on every one of the shoes, some twice. He walked around in them, jogged in place. He went back and forth among several brands before he finally selected two different types of Adidas—a heavier-soled training shoe and a lightweight kangaroo-skin racing shoe with spikes. He bounced the ultra-light red shoe in his hand, then took a deep sniff of the leather. The clerk finally returned to Tim, wondering if he had made a choice.

"These'll do, mate," said Tim. "Mr. Quigley said ye'd take care of me, so I'll take these two." As Tim placed the shoes in his bag, the inattentive clerk scratched his head and whispered, "Shit!" as he contemplated the charnel house of scattered, unselected shoes and the empty boxes he had to reassemble and reshelve.

"Sure. Whatever you say. You're all set," said the bewildered clerk.

"Thanks, mate. Cheers," said Tim. As the clerk began matching shoes with their empty boxes, Tim passed the unmanned checkout counter and exited the store.

The next morning, Tim entered the classroom more at ease than the previous few days. The bruises on his face had faded to a pale yellow, and his swollen lip had returned to its normal size. He took his seat and opened his literature text. Mr. Edwin Barnes, Tim's bearded and bespectacled English teacher, entered the room, placed his briefcase on the table, then scrawled "The Second Coming" on the chalkboard.

The poet, W. B. Yeats, was a familiar figure to Tim since he was a Sligo man, buried not far from the Connolly farm. Tim understood this poem well now, especially the part about "things falling apart."

As Mr. Barnes began to introduce the poem, Mrs. James, the ill-tempered school secretary, knocked at the door, her curling index finger drawing the teacher into the hallway. After listening to her for a moment, he returned to the classroom and adjusted his baggy brown sports jacket as he spoke.

"Mr. Connolly!"

Tim answered, "Yes, sir?"

"Brother Frank would like you to report to his office immediately."

Amidst low murmuring among the students, Cooper leaned over toward Tim.

"Looks like time for another ass-whipping, Paddy!" he said.

Ashen-faced and nervous, Tim gathered his books and left the room. Two minutes later, he found the office with "Athletic Director" embossed on the brass name plate.

Coach Quigley, farther down the hall, had just stepped out of the gym when he noticed Tim standing at the entrance of Brother Frank's office. Concerned, he stopped, then turned to follow him.

As Tim stood nervously in the doorway of the outer office, he noticed Brother Frank in the corner of a small room adjoining the office. He was kneeling before a statue of the Virgin Mary, head bowed, back to the door. He had rosary beads in his hands and whispered repetitive prayers. Then he stood and blessed himself with the small crucifix attached to the beads and kissed it. Tim thought he heard the softly murmured words, "Mother Mary, forgive me." Turning to face Tim, he appeared misty-eyed. He sniffed and blew his nose into a handkerchief.

"Have a seat, Mr. Connolly," he said. Tim sat in front of Brother Frank's desk. "Do you have any idea why you are here?"

"No, sir—uh, Brother," Tim stammered.

"I understand you were at Randy's Sporting Goods yesterday," said Brother Frank.

Confused, Tim said, "Yes, I needed running shoes. I joined the track team, and.—"

"Stop!" The brother stood and walked menacingly from behind his desk to sit on the front edge, directly before Tim. "In this country, Connolly, when we buy something, we pay for it."

Tim's brow furrowed when tried to speak. "But I—"

Brother Frank interrupted again. "I just got off the phone with the store owner, and apparently you just walked out without paying for your shoes."

Tim stood and sputtered, "But I was—"

Brother Frank said, "Sit back down, and be quiet till I tell you to speak." Tim sat. "You, Connolly, are nothing but a common thief."

Tim shook his head and tried to talk. "No, sir, I—"

"I said, shut your mouth till I tell you to speak," he repeated angrily. Then Brother Frank's face softened, and an odd grin replaced his scowl. He walked behind Tim and placed his backhand gently on the side of Tim's head. The boy squirmed, confused and agitated. "What'll your parents say when I call them?"

Not sure what was going on, Tim fidgeted uncomfortably in his seat. "They're not here, Brother," he said.

Quigley stood eavesdropping outside the athletic office.

"Where are they?" inquired the brother.

"Me Ma's in Ireland, working," said Tim.

"And your father? What's his story?"

Tim remained silent. Brother Frank moved to his side. His left leg brushed against Tim's. Tim cringed, increasingly confused and discomfited. "I said, what's his story?" repeated Brother Frank.

Tim muttered, "He's in prison."

"Another common thief, no doubt. This must run in your family," the brother whispered, goading Tim. He now positioned himself in front of the seated boy. Tim snorted bitterly and clenched his fists. He glared at Brother Frank with hate in his eyes.

"Don't you dare look at me like that. You're a slow learner, aren't you, boy? Stand up." Reluctantly, Tim stood. Quigley entered the office unseen.

"Maybe this will instill some wisdom," said Brother Frank as he cocked arm to strike Tim.

The coach stepped forward, adroitly grabbed Brother Frank's wrist, and restrained him.

"There's no need to strike the boy again, Brother," he said. "There has been some confusion here."

Brother Frank shook his arm loose and directed a hateful glance at Quigley.

"He just joined the track team yesterday," the coach continued. "I sent the boy to pick up proper running shoes and to tell Randy, the owner, that I would pay for them." Quigley turned to Tim. "Did you tell Randy I said to set you up?"

Tim moved several steps away from Brother Frank, who continued to stare at Quigley. "I told the lad who showed me the shoes," said Tim.

"There's the confusion," said Quigley. "Randy's an old friend. It was probably a clerk who didn't know the arrangement. I am paying for the boy's shoes. That was the deal."

Brother Frank, after staring at Quigley this whole time, turned to Tim.

"Okay, Connolly. Get out of here. I don't want to see you in here again." Tim looked at Quigley, then quickly left the office.

After the boy left, Quigley said, "I'm glad we could clear that up." But as he started to leave the office, Brother Frank stepped in front of him.

"Mr. Quigley. A word, please."

He paused, his face calm, his manner unruffled.

"Who the hell do you think you are," Brother Frank continued, "challenging me in front of a student?"

Quigley replied calmly, "You were about to hit an innocent boy. Don't you think you've battered him enough already?"

Trembling with anger, Brother Frank said, "Don't presume to tell me how to run things. I've been dealing with these boys for a long time!" He pointed a threatening finger at Quigley, about to say more, but stopped himself.

Comprehending the unspoken message, Quigley left the office.

Chapter Twenty-One

QUIGLEY WALKED UP A BUSY STREET of tall apartment houses, four blocks from the Long Island Expressway. He crossed the street where boys were playing stickball, tramping over long-buried trolley tracks that peered randomly through the worn asphalt like skeletal limbs creeping from graveyard slabs.

He climbed two flights of stairs and entered his dark, one-bedroom apartment, threw his briefcase and trench coat over a chair and flipped the living room light switch. On the wall behind him, a gallery of photos showed him in his younger days, breaking tapes at finish lines, holding trophies, and shaking hands with an older Jesse Owens. Tarnished trophies populated his mantle. Across the room, a table of family photos—him as a bridegroom with his bride, Linda, Captain Quigley in his Marine uniform, Quigley and his wife and their two small children, and later photos of the two children as young adults.

He turned on the TV, then selected a Swanson TV dinner from the freezer and placed it in the oven. After grabbing a bottle of Johnnie Walker Red from the cupboard, Quigley filled a tumbler and sat in front of the TV. He placed his feet on the coffee table and drained his glass. After watching CBS local news headlines for a few minutes, he switched to WPIX to watch an old episode of *Gunsmoke*. He contemplated his empty glass for a moment before approving a refill. On the coffee table, next to the whiskey bottle, sat a crumpled letter from his wife's attorney.

Chapter Twenty-Two

MEN IN DARK WOOLEN JACKETS AND CAPS and women in dark sweaters or shawls, heads covered with hats or kerchiefs, waited in single file outside the small Strandhill cottage in a heavy mist. Two men wearing black balaclava caps stood in front of the cottage with automatic weapons slung over their shoulders. Three elderly women in long black dresses, with black shawls draped over their heads, keened softly in the background.

Bridget, pale and drawn, waited in line behind friends and neighbors paying their respects to Veronica Cawley, whose son, Donal, had just died in an H-Block hunger strike. Mrs. Cawley received her visitors standing next to Donal's casket, his body neatly laid out in his fine, dark blue Sunday suit, hands folded over his chest, a rosary knitted in his waxy fingers. A vase of white, trumpet-shaped Easter lilies sat on the kitchen table, their sweet aroma at war with the bitter mood. The Cawley's gray-and-white-striped cat snaked among the visitors, rubbing his head and body on unsuspecting legs.

Bridget clutched her purse in her left hand as she briefly hugged Veronica and whispered her sorrow into her ear. Behind Bridget, the IRA man came in, removed his woolen cap, and scanned the room. Mourners in the queue separated as he approached Mrs. Cawley. He spoke a few hushed words to her, then placed a folded Irish flag in her hands. Bridget's composure faltered at that point, and she began to tremble.

A neighbor tried to lead her to a chair, but she opted to leave the cottage. She walked a short distance in the misty rain before she fell to her knees, sobbing uncontrollably. Maeve Grogan, who had been commiserating with Donal's father, noticed Bridget's distress. She excused herself and followed her. Kneeling, she placed her arm around Bridget's shoulder.

"Bridget, love," she said, "Have yourself a good cry. Ye've more than ample reason, I'd say."

She nodded and slowly gathered herself. Maeve then took Bridget's elbow and helped her to her feet. "Listen to me," she said. "We've been over this before. Come with me. Let's get out of this rain and get a snug at Duffy's before the crowd from Veronica's packs in. You and I, we need to talk some more."

Bridget smiled weakly. "Sure, why not?" They walked the short distance to Duffy's and settled into the snug with the stain-glassed window in the far corner of the pub.

"Sean," Maeve called to the bartender, "bring us two Powers—doubles, neat. That's a good lad."

"Goodness," Bridget sighed, "sure and I'll be havin' me own wake after one of them."

Maeve ignored her concern and began her homily.

"Once again, it's time for us women to off our arses. We can't just sit back, weeping and feckin wailing. Stop me if I'm repeating meself. Uh. . .on second thought, no, don't." She continued, "Listen, we've our own bloody work to do. And I mean work. There is increasing anger, outrage even, from women on both sides of the border with what's taking place in Belfast. They all want this to stop, but their useless husbands and the bloodthirsty politicians—those goddam eegits—are so consumed with their macho 'eye for an eye' bullshit that nothing ever gets done."

Maeve paused to throw back her drink, then waved to Sean and swirled her arm for another. "So far, we have developed a network of some one hundred and fifty women on both sides of the border." She laughed. "A network! Ah, Jaysus, I don't think I've ever used that word. Anyway, a feckin network! Our plan is to catalogue all the known abuse to our men and make it public. We are organizing protest marches. We will be sending letters to the union leaders and newspaper editors, writing our own columns, notifying the TV stations when we are going to raise bloody hell, and then we are going to march outside the Dail in Dublin and Stormont in Belfast, so they know we mean business."

Bridget nodded enthusiastically. "Yes. Absolutely. I'll do everything I can, Maeve. Count me in."

After Sean delivered Maeve's whiskey, Maeve handed Bridget a small black pad from her purse.

"Here's a list of our planned activities and events. Sign on for as many as ye can, and the arse kicking will begin." She raised her glass and said, "Slainte!"

"Slainte," said Bridget, tapping Maeve's glass.

Chapter Twenty-Three

OVER THE NEXT WEEK, TIM SETTLED into a stable academic and athletic routine. On Monday morning, he was in class taking notes, raising his hand, answering questions. That afternoon, Tim sprinted up the homestretch as Quigley shouted his lap time. On the rainy Tuesday that followed, Tim and his teammates worked out in the gym—lifting weights and doing sit-ups, pull-ups, and push-ups. Tim had added five pounds of muscle to his slender frame since school had begun.

That night, Tim did his homework at the kitchen table while Mary and Gary watched TV. On Wednesday, he and the team did a long-distance workout, running wooded hills and trails in Forest Park. Wednesday night, Tim chatted with his aunt and uncle about his classes and his workouts. On Thursday, Quigley held time trials for the team. He stood at the finish line as Tim crossed; pressing his stopwatch, he smiled approvingly.

After the time trials, Quigley gathered the team near the starting line.

"Well, gentlemen," he said, "this was our final preparation for Saturday's two-mile relay. Now remember: The eight-hundred-meter run may be the most demanding race in track." He paused for effect. "You need speed *and* endurance. But you need this too," he said, pointing to his head. "Pace yourself. Make sure you have some strength in reserve for the finish." Quigley looked at each of them intently. "Also, you need this," he said, pointing to his heart.

"This is what separates the losers from the winners. Any questions?"

There were none.

"See you Saturday morning. Rest up."

Tim eased off his spikes and put on his sweats and training shoes, then jogged away by himself.

Quigley studied Tim as he retreated. He was anxious to see how the young man would respond to the pressure of running in his first major competition, especially the anchor leg of the relay. Then he checked his clipboard, looked at his watch, and went home.

As Tim jogged by the shot-put circle on his way to the locker room, he noticed a tall, muscular girl putting the shot. She circled the tight ring with a certain swift violence, then grunted ferociously as she propelled the steel ball in the air.

Tim stopped and watched her through a chain-link fence. When she saw him gawking at her, she challenged him.

"What the hell are you lookin at?

Caught off guard, he sputtered, "Sorry, lass. You. Very impressive. Ye've got a lot of power."

She squinted at him and growled, "No shit. Who the hell are you? You ain't from around here."

Tim chuckled. "No. That's for sure. Tim Connolly. You?"

"Regina Carbone. Gina," she said, sounding suspicious.

"Gina. Grand. Cheers!" said Tim.

Gina Carbone was a two-time Catholic high school champion in the shot put, discus, and javelin. She was being scouted, from one competition to the next, by college coaches who recognized her national-class potential and the sought-for Title IX compliance athlete. Gina had long, dark curly hair that she wore in a tight bun during her workouts. She had a smooth Mediterranean complexion and a stolid, unsmiling face. She stood six feet tall and had a shapely 170-pound frame, one that featured broad shoulders, a muscular back, legs, thighs, and prominent breasts. Despite her athletic accomplishments and notoriety, Gina was not popular with either the female or the male students. She considered most of the girls insipid, or "hopelessly stupid" in her words. She considered the boys to be "morons" and "dumbasses," and was not shy about letting any of them know exactly how she regarded them.

Not surprisingly, Gina had no friends. Her size and her temperament intimidated people and prevented her from fitting into any clique, but she seemed fine with that. She was a decent student in math and science, though she had little patience with social studies and English. Only someone who didn't know her would have had the temerity to engage her in conversation.

###

Gina grinned fiendishly at Tim as she rubbed chalk on her hand and bounced another steel ball in her hand.

"You're the Irish kid those morons hate," she said.

Tim wondered what she knew. "What do you mean?"

"Mean?" she repeated. "You kidding? Just watch yourself, Greenhorn."

Gina stepped back into the circle and leaned sideways, shifting her weight over her right foot, the steel ball pressed against her neck, under her right ear. She coiled like a rattlesnake about to strike, then suddenly exploded in a double spin to the wooden edge of the circle, firing her steel projectile like a human cannon. Leaving the circle and breathing heavily, Gina clapped the chalk off her hands and looked again at Tim.

"You still here? Well, as I was sayin', I hear them talkin'. For some reason, Cooper hates you. Watch yourself. This Cooper's an evil prick. I know that because he spends a lot of time here practicing the shot. I have to listen to his bragging and bullshitting all the time. And his two stupid friends ain't much better. They just follow him around like a couple of dumbass puppies." Gina unwrapped two sticks of chewing gum, placed them in her mouth and began chewing. She offered a stick to Tim.

He shook his head. "No thanks." Then he said, "Thanks for the advice. I'll watch them. What's this Cooper's problem anyway? It's not just me. He seems to hate everybody."

Gina turned away and placed her equipment into a gym bag, answering offhandedly.

"Problem?" she said. "How's this? His old man comes home drunk one night. Shoots the mother, then puts the barrel in his mouth and shoots himself. With a shotgun. A real fucking mess. Big news here about four years ago."

Tim's eyes widened. "Jaysus! No wonder he's a bloody nutter! Still . . . kind of sad when you think about it."

Gina released her hair and shrugged.

"Yeah, sad. I guess. They sent him to a nuthouse for a while, but it didn't do no good. Made him worse, in fact." She turned her head and spat out her gum. Looking back at Tim, she changed the subject. "I'm watchin' you run, kiddo. You got speed. You train right, you'll do good."

Tim thanked her. They looked at each other for a moment, and the conversation stalled.

"Well, I'll be off then," he said as he shuffled backward. See you around, Gina. Cheers."

"Yeah. *Cheers*," she replied, having never used that phrase in her life. She watched Tim as he walked away, whispering to herself, "What a goofball."

###

John Cooper had learned mean at an early age. His father, Jake, was a red-faced, overweight New York City vice cop with a bad attitude and a violent reputation. Numerous complaints of battery and sexual assault had been filed against him during his fifteen-year career. Many of these complaints were dismissed summarily since the complainants were usually prostitutes or pimps. Later in his career, however, he was suspended after he and his partner raided a private dance club in Astoria, where sex and drugs shared equal billing with the rock-and-roll. Jake got excessively rough one night with an eighteen-year-old boy who happened to be the nephew of the police commissioner.

The precinct knew little about Jake's family and couldn't have cared less. Other than telling his cohorts the usual macho jokes about his ball-breaking wife and his knuckleheaded son, he kept his private life private. He didn't share with anyone his frequent drunken abuse of them—those fearful domestic moments when an innocent or ill-timed word might send him into rage, swiping dishes off the table, then throwing punches at his wife and son or whipping them with his belt.

John Cooper had endured this regimen of abuse from his early years. As he reached adolescence and became bigger and stronger with his athletic training, he thought he might stand his ground one night to protect himself and his mother. During his freshman year at St. Jude's, he attempted to do just that.

It turned out to be a mistake. He hadn't accounted for his father's still-superior strength and long experience hitting people of all sizes and sexes, nor had he accounted for the sheer pleasure it gave the man. He beat his son mercilessly, even breaking his jaw.

When Cooper arrived at school in this condition two days after the event, Brother Frank reported Jake to his supervisors. This event dovetailed with the abuse of the commissioner's nephew, and Jake was fired. That night, he turned in his badge and his service revolver. After leaving the station, he bought a fifth of bourbon, drove to an empty section of the Roosevelt Field, and emptied the bottle. Jake pulled his personal revolver from his glove compartment, intending to "eat his gun," in the cop vernacular.

After placing the pistol in his mouth, though, Jake had a better idea. He decided to take his wife and son with him. When he arrived home, he retrieved his shotgun from the garage and staggered into the kitchen. He confronted his terrified wife, blamed her for his miserable fate, and shot her to death. He looked for his son, but John snuck up behind him, smashed a wooden chair over his head, and ran out of the house. Within thirty seconds, John heard the second shot. His father had turned the shotgun on himself.

When John was brought into custody by the police, he was so disoriented that Social Services was called in, and they placed him under observation at the Queens County Hospital. He spent thirty days in the psych ward before he was released into the custody of his mother's sister and her husband. They accepted him grudgingly, and only after acceding to a favorable financial settlement from his parents' estate.

The living arrangement was tense, harsh, and aggravated by Cooper's growing antisocial behavior and blatant, often profane, disrespect for his penurious guardians. The arrangement improved slightly as Cooper got older and spent less time at their home, given his active participation in football, where his rage found expression. Even there, though, he was often flagged for unsportsmanlike conduct, and once suspended for three games during his sophomore season for excessive violence—kicking a downed opponent into unconsciousness after a play had ended.

Chapter Twenty-Four

MARY, SEATED AT THE KITCHEN TABLE, held a letter in one hand and a handkerchief in the other, dabbing her eyes.

Gary had arrived home later than usual. Still wearing his black Kevlar coat and heavy, shin-high structural boots, he thumped noisily into the apartment. His face was blackened with soot. Weary, he threw his coat over a closet door, then slumped into a chair to remove his mud-splattered boots.

"We had a bad one today, Mary," he said. "A five-alarm mess in Williamsburg, two buildings collapsed, eight people . . ." He stopped when he noticed that she was weeping. "Jesus Christ. Now what?"

She waved the letter. "I just got this from Bridget," she replied. "Things are not good. And watch your language, please, for pity's sake! Terence has joined the hunger strike. He's been . . ."

"I'm sorry, Mary, that's awful," he said.

"Ten days with no food. Gary, nine of these men have already died . . . Me poor sister's at her wit's end. She can't even see him now. He's off in some separate wing." Mary pulled away and went to the window. "And she's missin' her boy somethin terrible. I feel so helpless."

"Mary, this is awful, I know, but we're already doing all we can. What else—"

Mary interrupted, "How can we tell him about his father?"

"We're not going to. Not yet. He don't need no more trouble.

He's just starting to act—I don't know, normal?"

Mary sat and tried to compose herself. She crumpled the letter in her fist.

"This boy, Gary, I don't know. He's upset your life . . . our life, I know. Still, somehow, I feel responsible. Like maybe if we're patient . . . I don't know, maybe he'll come around?"

Gary smiled, appreciating his wife's gentle nature but unconvinced by her optimism.

"If he does, that will be wonderful, but it's been a rough going so far. I'll try harder with the kid. Maybe that'll help. But he's a tough case."

Chapter Twenty-Five

YELLOW SCHOOL BUSES, VANS, and hundreds of cars filled the stadium parking lot. Off-duty police were directing traffic into orderly rows and open spaces. Athletes, students, parents, fans, college coaches, and local reporters filtered through the turnstiles as field speakers blared in the background.

The first Saturday of every March, the Iona Relays kicked off the beginning of the outdoor track season. Runners from all the New York City high schools were warming up around the entire track—jogging, stretching, some rubbing pungent wintergreen lineament on their calves, hamstrings, and thighs, others gulping Gatorade. The men's toilet was busy with long lines of nervous runners tending to their agitated bowels and bladders.

Coach Quigley gathered Tim, Blake, and the other two members of their relay team in a far corner of the track.

"We've got about thirty minutes before our race," he said, "so warm up, stretch, and be back here in twenty minutes. Be sure you practice passing the baton like we did in our workouts." Tim and his relay mates laced up their spikes and began stretching and jogging in the infield grass. Tim noticed Gina on the other side of the field near the shot-put circle. He whistled and shouted to her.

"Hey! Gina!" When she turned around, he grinned and flashed a thumbs-up.

Gina grimaced, embarrassed.

"Oh, for Christ's sake," she whispered to herself. She looked around her area to make sure no one was watching, then surreptitiously returned a thumbs-up, rolling her eyes while straining to suppress a smile. "Goofball" she muttered.

Minutes before their race, Quigley reassembled his team for last-minute instructions. Wally Mason and Sid Johnson were the two other members of the relay team joining Tim and Blake. While Tim, Wally, and Sid paid close attention to the coach, Blake sported a distant, almost bored, expression on his face.

"This should be an exciting race," Quigley said. "St. Francis Prep is a city powerhouse, and they usually have their best team in this relay." He put a hand on Wally's shoulder and said, "Wally, first leg. Give us a good strong pace, stay as close as you can to the leader and make sure you get the baton to Sid, here, the way we practiced it. Sid, you also, keep it as close as possible. Relax going out, so you don't tie up at the end. If that lactic acid kicks in, you'll think you were hit by a truck." Quigley checked his clipboard, then turned to Blake. "Tyrone, you'll probably have to make up some ground on St. Francis, but knowing what you're capable of, I expect you to give the baton to Tim with a lead."

Finally, he gave Tim a fierce look and said, "Tim, this is your chance. Don't hold back." He gathered his team in a circle. "Okay, men. Let's have a good race." They put their hands together, and the coach lowered his head, "Our Lady of Victory . . ."

The team responded, "pray for us."

Just then, the field speaker blared, "Will the teams for the two-mile relay please come to the starting line?" As St. Jude's two-mile relay team moved to the starting line, Tim noticed Blake scanning the crowd. He watched his teammate until he made eye contact with Cooper. Cooper saluted and smiled at Blake, who nodded his head in return.

Tim remembered what Gina had told him.

Tyrone Blake was one of twenty-two black students out of St. Jude's student population of 750. Tall and wiry-strong with a handsome, sensitive, unsmiling face, he'd enrolled at St. Jude's after Brother Frank noticed him at a Catholic Youth Organization camp when he was ten years old. He was, even as a child, a skilled athlete in baseball and basketball. But his exceptional foot speed set him apart from the other boys his age. Brother Frank wanted him at St. Jude's, so he made a determined effort to recruit him, visiting his home, charming his parents, and winning them over with the promise of free tuition and special attention.

A popular figure when he first arrived at St. Jude's, Blake was recruited by Father Kenney in his freshman year to join the school's sodality, a religious club dedicated to St. Jude, believing that he might eventually be recruited into their religious order as a priest or brother. After two years, Father Kenney thought a priestly vocation was a possibility, especially after Blake had attended several retreats at an upstate monastery.

However, once Blake was spotted at his Junior Prom "dirty dancing" and French kissing a female student, Father Kenney abandoned that pursuit. Brother Frank, on the other hand, continued to pursue Blake for his own reasons.

###

All seven teams assembled near the starting line. The first-leg runners came to the line, each in his individual lane. Wally took his place in the third lane. On the perimeter, Sid, Blake, and Tim shook their arms, stretched their legs, and jogged in place, trying to stay loose. Standing on his podium, the starter shouted.

"Gentlemen. On your mark!"

The runners leaned forward on the starting line.

"Get set!"

The starter then raised his pistol and fired in the air. As the runners sprinted off the line, confined within their staggered lanes, they entered a self-contained, isolated world for the next two-plus minutes. The St. Francis team in lane one easily took the lead. Wally was in fourth place but managed to stay within fifteen meters of the leader. As Wally finished his leg, he held fourth place and flawlessly passed the baton to Sid. The shouting from the team members and the crowd increased in volume and intensity. Sid went out fast and quickly passed the third man. He moved up on the second-place runner, down the far stretch of the first lap. As he made the final turn, near the seven-hundred-meter mark, Sid made a move to overtake the leader, but he tightened up, fell back, and was twenty meters behind the St. Francis runner and in third place when he passed the baton to Blake.

Blake started out in a hurry and quickly gained ground on the second-place runner. He kept a smooth, long stride behind him until he reached the four-hundred-meter mark, at which point he took second place. He held this position until the final turn, when he passed the St. Francis runner with a powerful burst. Seeing this, Tim moved into the inside lane, anticipating Blake's baton pass. In the final fifty meters, firmly in the lead, Blake sped toward Tim, who was waiting for the baton, looking straight ahead with his right arm extended behind him. However, as Blake entered the passing lane, he let the baton slip from his hand just before reaching Tim. The baton bounced into the next lane. The St. Francis runner entering that lane accidentally kicked it to the outermost lane of the track. Scattered groans echoed in the bleachers. Quigley cursed and slammed his clipboard to the ground. In the bleachers, Cooper beamed.

Tim instinctively ran out of his lane, retrieved the baton, and shouted at Blake.

"Ye feckin 'git'."

A track official pointed at Tim and shouted, "St. Jude is disqualified,"

Tim ignored him and took off after the pack, which had left him far behind in last place. By the middle of his first lap, Tim had closed the gap. He was running strong and smooth. His face and body were relaxed, his mind focused only on the runner in front of him. And the next one. And the next one. By the end of the first lap, he'd passed all but the leader, the St. Francis star who still had a commanding twenty-five-meter lead.

He looked back, saw Tim at some distance, and settled confidently into a steady pace. With just over two hundred meters to go, Tim accelerated. He strode powerfully to the right shoulder of the St. Francis runner.

One hundred to go. Quigley was screaming and waving his clipboard wildly. Sid and Wally ran to the edge of the track to cheer Tim. Blake watched silently, sitting in the grass, as he pulled on his sweats.

As the crowd cheered, Tim paced the St. Francis runner, stride for stride until, with fifty meters to go, he kicked into a higher gear, surging past his stunned opponent. Then unexpectedly, just before he hit the tape, Tim veered off the track and handed his baton to the race official. The St. Francis runner, who'd been fifteen meters behind by that point, broke the tape as the winner.

Blake skulked away from the track toward the locker room. He looked toward Cooper in the bleachers, who gave him a disgusted wave. Quigley caught up with Tim, bent over, still breathing heavily.

"Great race, son. Amazing. You showed me something special. And everybody else too."

Angry, he asked, "Where's Blake?"

"Don't worry about him," said Quigley. "I'll talk to him. You just cool down and hit the shower. We'll talk later."

Sid and Wally patted Tim on the back and congratulated him. The St. Francis runner whom Tim had outdistanced jogged over briefly, grabbed Tim's hand, and smiled.

"You're something else, man. Unreal," he said. He took off before Tim had a chance to thank him.

Tim retrieved his sweats and sat down on the infield grass, removing his spikes. He was just catching his breath when a middle-aged gentleman, nattily attired in a dark green woolen blazer, tan slacks, and penny loafers approached him.

"Got a minute, son? I'm Marvin Stewart, sports reporter with the *Long Island Press*. That was quite a race you just ran."

Tim grinned. "Thank ye, sir."

"Do I detect an Irish accent?" Stewart asked.

"Yes, indeed."

Stewart said, "I'd like to run a story on you."

"Ye'r kidding, eh?" Tim grabbed his spikes and stood up.

"Not at all. Tell me some things about yourself, like where you're from, why you're here . . . that sort of thing."

Tim looked around for his coach and waved to him. Quigley came over and shook hands with Stewart.

"Mr. Stewart here would like to do a story on me," said Tim.

"Mr. Stewart! Pleased to meet you," said Quigley. "Always enjoy your columns and TV work."

"And I remember you very well, Mr. Quigley," said Stewart. "You had quite an amazing career in the late forties, early fifties."

The coach raised his eyebrows. "Thanks. I'm surprised anyone remembers anymore."

"Sorry about the ways things ended," said Stewart.

"Well, you know . . . all good things," said Quigley drily. "But how about this young man, here? He's quite special." Stewart turned to Tim, and the interview continued for nearly fifteen minutes. Throughout, Tim didn't mention his parents' desperate plight nor his forced exile, choosing instead to call his visit with his American relatives a "cultural experience."

Tim and Quigley then shook hands with Stewart and said goodbye. As they were walking away, the reporter shouted after them.

"Hey Tim! One last question: *Why* do you run?"

Tim smiled and shouted back, "Coach, here, asked me."

"No, seriously. I'm curious." Stewart paced over to where Tim and Quigley now stood.

"Seriously?" echoed Tim. This simple question startled him. His smile disappeared like the sun behind a cloud, and a darkness altered his voice. He looked at Stewart, then Quigley, and he answered slowly, deliberately. "When I run, I'm alone. And I'm free. No one can touch me." He took a deep breath and shook his head, "No one." Tim turned to Quigley. "Right, Coach?"

Quigley read the anger in Tim's hardened eyes and answered.

"That's right, Tim." With that, they finished their interview and thanked Stewart again. Tim then jogged toward the locker room.

Unseen through all of this, Brother Frank lurked in the shadows at the top step of the bleachers near the press box, glaring down like a medieval gargoyle. Tight-lipped and seething, he had been watching the whole exchange.

Chapter Twenty-Six

"HEY GREENHORN!" GINA SHOUTED as Tim headed toward the locker room. He waited for her. "Nice race," she said.

"Thanks. How'd ye do?" Tim inquired.

"You need to ask?" she grinned, brandishing her gold medal. She placed her hands on her hips and spoke in a darker tone. "I warned you about them pricks, didn't I?" Reaching into her equipment bag, she retrieved a shiny red apple. "I got another. Want one?"

Tim declined.

"Indeed, ye did, Gina. I saw them." Tim curled his lip in anger. "Just before the race. Like ye said, I figured they were up to something."

"Mopes," she said. She took a giant bite out of her apple. Too big. Turning her head away from Tim, she spat out a large chunk and coughed before she spoke. "People are fucked up. It's important to know who your enemies are. Especially you, around here," she said, gesturing toward the track, "with these goons." She wiped her mouth with the sleeve of her sweatshirt and spit out a last apple seed.

They started walking back toward the field house and locker rooms.

Tim said soberly, "That's true everywhere. Ireland too, ya know?"

"Yeah. I seen them bombings and all on TV. A lot of people getting killed over there. You into that?"

Tim kept his voice quiet. "No. Not me."

Gina asked, "What's it like where you're from? Not all these buildings and cars and people, I bet."

"Ye'd be right about that," said Tim. "So, what's it like? Well . . . outside Sligo town, where I live, it's mostly pasture. Hills and meadows. Sheep and some cattle grazing on the slopes. Lots of fishing boats in the harbor. Near the coast, there's this impressive old castle."

Gina listened with curiosity, trying to imagine that such places still existed.

"Sure, and every day the ocean breezes keep the weather changing. Some rain almost every day—misty rain, soft rain, hard rain, and some days just plain rain." He laughed. "Summer nights are long and lazy. Winter days are short, very short, cold, and damp."

"Sounds pretty goddam boring," Gina said. "And backwards. And you miss this?"

Tim lowered his head. "Aye, indeed I do."

"Then why the hell are you here and not back there?" she inquired.

"Long story. Another time, eh?"

They arrived at the field house, and Tim said, "Well, good talking with ye. I guess I'll be seeing ye around."

"Yeah," Gina said. As Tim started to walk away, she called to him. "Oh, one more thing." He stopped and turned. Gina smiled in an unexpectedly girlish manner. "Speaking of 'another time,' there's a school dance in two weeks. I never go to the damn things. Always seemed kinda stupid. But I'd like to go to this one."

Tim missed her overture and remained silent.

"With *you*, dingleberry!" she exclaimed. "Jesus! Are all the Irish as slow as you?"

Tim responded as if shaken from a nap and smiled.

"Okay. Sure. Yeah." He clapped his spikes together and beamed. "Yeah. Sure. Brilliant!" He backed away slowly, wearing a wide grin, not sure what else to say. "Okay, so I guess I'll talk to you . . . during the week, eh? Cheers, then."

"Yeah. Cheers," said Gina, shaking her head and laughing. They started walking in separate directions, but then Gina stopped and turned to watch him. As though feeling her eyes, Tim looked back at her and waved.

Chapter Twenty-Seven

TIM ENTERED THE APARTMENT in a cheerful mood. He placed his equipment bag on the floor and greeted his aunt and uncle. Then he went to the refrigerator and grabbed a milk carton. Mary didn't turn around, just peered out the window while wringing a dishtowel.

"How did it go today, Tim?" she inquired.

"Fine," he said, struggling to hide his satisfaction. He poured a tall glass of milk. "A strange day, but things went all right, I think."

Mary turned away from him to mask her emotion.

"What's wrong, Aunt Mary?" he asked.

Gary came in from the next room and noticed his wife near tears.

"Mary?" He reached for her, but she turned to Tim. Gary's attempt to intervene failed as Mary blurted the hunger strike news to Tim.

The boy grabbed the edge of the chair in disbelief.

"What?" he said. "What?" He stared at his hands, shaking his head. "No . . . no. Not that," he whispered.

Mary gathered herself. "Your Da needs our prayers now more than ever." Tim was not listening. He walked to the window, staring out in silence, then started to tremble.

"I must be goin' home. I can't be here now," he said. Mary walked to his side and put her arm around his shoulder. Tim stood, motionless, shoulders slumped. Gary interjected, commiserating with Tim while telling him that they would honor any decision he made.

"Just think it through carefully," said Gary. "In the meantime, you are entirely welcome to continue here with us." His sudden mild tone surprised Tim. The boy shrugged his shoulders, not sure what to say.

When he entered his room, Tim noticed that a picture of his father, his mother, and himself had been added to the photos of his cousin. Tim looked in the closet and saw that it had been emptied of his cousin's old clothes, sports gear, and army uniform. Touched by this gesture, Tim walked back into the living room, where his aunt and uncle stood still, watching him. Gary extended his hands and seemed about to say something but stopped. He coughed and swallowed.

"I thought you could use the space," he said quietly. Tim nodded his appreciation with tears in his eyes. Then he returned to his room, sat at his desk, and tore a piece of paper from his notebook. Pen in hand, he began writing.

Da, I just heard about your hunger strike. Please don't do this. I want you to come home to Ma. I'm afraid of what's happening. I feel like I'm in jail, like you. I want you to come home. And I want to come home. I want our old life back. Love, your son, Tim

Chapter Twenty-Eight

MILLIE SNORED QUIETLY ON HER PLAID woolen blanket near the hearth. While Bridget sat at the kitchen table, tapping the keys on a borrowed Olympia portable typewriter, a tea kettle whistled impatiently, venting steam. A large sheaf of papers—letters, files, news clippings—lay to the left of the typewriter. Finished copy lay to the right: letters written to local, county, and national newspaper and television editors, union leaders, and politicians. The letters would be dropped in the post this morning, the opening salvo of Maeve's "network." Scores of interviews with affected families and some former prisoners had produced an impressive portfolio on H-Block's human rights abuses. Their two months of work had begun to show results.

Bridget expected Maeve shortly, and they would be joining a Belfast caravan to demonstrate in solidarity with Catholic women from the North. Their plan was to rally in Belfast that afternoon at a juncture near the Prince of Wales Avenue and begin the one-mile march to the Parliament buildings on the Stormont estate.

Bridget had contacted her neighbor, Bess, with care instructions regarding Millie and the livestock, given the likelihood she would be gone for more than a day. Just as Bridget poured the hot water into her teacup, she heard Maeve's auto from a distance. The woman was a notoriously reckless driver and had terrified many unsuspecting travelers on Sligo's narrow roads. Maeve's car presently tore up Bridget's long gravel driveway, zigzagging at an alarming speed, scattering three frightened sheep. Bridget gathered her overnight bag and her letters and papers, then opened the front door just after Maeve hit the brakes in a cloud of gravel and dust. Leaning on her horn, she greeted Bridget lustily.

"Bridget, me dear, this is going to be a big feckin deal. We've got papers and TV coverage from all over the country, even some from America."

Once she was in the car, Bridget told Maeve that she had received unexpected news yesterday from Terence's grandfather, Brian.

"Can ye believe this wild old man is working with IRA groups in Armagh? Anyway, he heard of our work, mentioned it to a few of his local commanders, and they will be making regular donations to our effort."

"That's grand," said Maeve. "We can certainly use it every bit of it . . . Well, enough chit-chat. Let's be gone." She floored the accelerator, anxious to join the Belfast caravan. The sheep had safely relocated to an adjoining field.

Chapter Twenty-Nine

AS TIM WALKED THE HALLS to Quigley's office, random students congratulated him; some patted him on the back and said, "Great race!" He acknowledged them distractedly.

When Tim entered his office, Quigley set aside the sheaf of papers he was collating and stapling. He set his stapler next to the photo of his wife and two children and greeted his star runner with a wide grin.

"Amazing run Saturday, Tim. You created quite a stir. I've had three calls from college coaches. Did you see the morning paper?"

Tim shook his head. "No, sir."

Quigley pushed the paper across his desk. "Stewart did a nice piece on you. Headline: 'The Boy from Mullaghmore Steals the Show at the Iona Relays'."

Tim was unresponsive.

"What's wrong, Tim? I thought you'd be excited with all this."

"I am, sir. It's just . . . well . . . I must be goin' home." Tim strained to speak. "Me ma's in a bad way what with me father and all." Tim took a seat and rubbed his face. Quigley came from behind his desk, his cheerful mood turned sour.

"Tell me what's wrong, son."

"Me Da's near dyin'," said Tim, struggling to keep calm. "Me mother's out of sorts, near broke, and doesn't know what to do."

"Tim," said the coach, "I'm so sorry. I knew there was some trouble, but I had no idea it was this bad."

Tim stood, turning his back. "Besides, I don't fit in here. I belong with me own people."

Quigley wasn't sure what to say. He struggled for words to reach Tim's pain and, at the same time, comprehend the sudden inexplicable stress that had seized him.

"Tim, this is dreadful. You have every reason to feel . . . ah, but . . . but—" Quigley stopped to catch his breath, wanting to proceed slowly. "Please, don't do anything rash now. Let's reflect on this before you make a final decision."

The coach walked back and forth, pushing his fingers through his hair and rubbing the back of his neck. "I can understand your desperate urge to be at home with your mom. Look, maybe I can help. Give me your mother's name and address. I'll write her."

Quigley handed Tim a pencil and a piece of paper. Tim scribbled the information on the paper and returned it.

"Now, Tim, let's think about this. What could you actually *do* if you went home? What are your options? Work? Possibly. But it's doubtful you could make enough money to make a difference, and you'd be mortgaging your own bright future here. And, sure, while your mother would be happy to see you, she might also need this time to concentrate on getting your father out of prison."

Quigley sat down, then stood again, pacing, and struggling to come up with good reasons, better reasons, to keep Tim from leaving. After another pause, he turned to Tim, inspired.

"Have you considered the possibility that you might do more good right here, you know, by winning races and getting your father's story in the press? You're 'The Boy from Mullaghmore!' You've already introduced your small Irish town to people in America." Quigley held up the newspaper and smacked it. "Proof!

Tim, I'm serious, you could be a major champion. You get the word out! People will pay attention. Listen, you've got a rare God-given talent. It'd be a sin not to develop it. And remember what you said to the reporter, Tim?" Quigley pointed to the paper. "Running made you free? Most of us spend our lives looking for what you have. It's here for you, right now, Tim." He paused and repeated passionately, "Tim, it's here. Right now."

Now his words turned darker, scalded by memory. "Your chance may never come again." Quigley waited for Tim to process this, then said offhandedly, "Ask yourself this: What would your father want you to do?"

Tim deliberated, then acknowledged Quigley's reasoning with a slight nod.

"Me Da?" He was fighting back tears. "Me Da? I'm not sure . . . but ye may be right, Coach." Tim's voice was hoarse. "I think . . . yeah, he would want me to stay here and fight."

"Okay, then," Quigley said. "Then that's what we'll do. Stay here and fight. We start in earnest today." He extended his hand to Tim, and Tim clasped it.

Chapter Thirty

TIM LEFT QUIGLEY'S OFFICE AND HEADED for the locker room. He tried the door, but it was locked. Reluctantly, he went to the athletic director's office to get a key, but Brother Frank wasn't there.

Noticing an open door to the locker room on the far side of the office, Tim walked through, sat at his locker, and changed into his running gear. As he headed for the track, he heard noises, heavy breathing coming from the shower room. Getting closer, he saw a misty reflection in the steamed mirror of the adjacent lavatory. Two naked bodies pressed against each other. Two blurred images quickly took shape in the steamy mirror. One was Blake. The other was Brother Frank.

Tim staggered backward.

"Jaysus. Bloody hell," Tim murmured.

Blake heard his voice, panicked, grabbed a towel, and staggered from the shower. Tim rushed out of the locker room, through the gym, and ran toward the track. He stopped before he reached it. Leaning against the chain-link fence, Tim tried to gather his breath and his thoughts.

Quigley saw him from the track and shouted.

"Tim! Let's go. What are you waiting for?"

"Be there in a minute, Coach," said Tim.

Moments later, Blake wearing his sweatsuit with a towel around his neck, bolted from the gym. Breathing heavily, his hair still wet and barefoot, he approached Tim.

"Connolly—I . . . Let me explain," he muttered in anguish.

Tim raised his hands in front of him and shook his head. "No . . . No."

"You've got to understand. I—"

"Understand? Understand? Are ye feckin kiddin me?" exclaimed Tim.

Quigley shouted from the track.

"Move it, you two!" Tim turned away and sprinted to the track. Blake walked back toward the locker room, his trembling hands pressed against his head.

Chapter Thirty-One

AT THE RALLY IN BELFAST, MAEVE and Bridget joined more than 150 women in the chill air and heavy mist. When the bullhorn blared at noon, they began their slow march on Stormont. Carrying anti-H-Block and anti-war signs, they chanted their grievances against the deplorable conditions in the prison and the violations of the prisoners' human rights. They also denounced the ceaseless sectarian violence that had been tearing Northern Ireland apart and killing thousands. Mothers and wives, sisters and daughters of men slain or imprisoned, all marched, demanding justice and peace. They sang familiar anthems urging peace and understanding. Along Prince of Wales Avenue, pockets of young male Loyalists jeered and shouted obscenities at the women; some pelted them with eggs and ripe tomatoes.

"Wretched little shits," Maeve called them.

Unexpectedly, hundreds more women, and men as well, joined the protesters and rallied with them as they marched through the Stormont Estate and the lavish grounds of the Parliament buildings. At numerous checkpoints, television reporters from BBC and ITV button-holed and questioned marchers, eager to tell their stories and raise public interest and support. Bridget and Maeve stopped to be interviewed three separate times.

After the interviews and the day's protests, a dignified, silver-haired man in a well-tailored black cashmere suit approached

Maeve and Bridget. He introduced himself in a professorial manner as Avery Donnellon.

"And how may we help you, Mr. Donnellon?" asked Maeve in her most pleasant voice.

"May I first say, ladies, congratulations to you and your colleagues on your rally today. I know how difficult these events are to manage, but you did a truly amazing job and raised a lot of eyebrows."

"And whose eyebrows would they be, Mr. Donnellon?" asked Bridget.

"Well, not only mine, of course, but also those of Owen Carron, a prominent member with the Sinn Fein party. He is very concerned, like you, with the terrible treatment of the H-Block prisoners. In fact, he formed an anti-H-Block committee in Northern Ireland last year that helped elect hunger striker Bobby Sands to the British Parliament. Owen Carron himself is Bobby's agent and took the seat as his proxy. As I said, he was quite impressed with your showing today and would like to meet with you later about the possibility of speaking with him at a formal press conference tomorrow. To be direct, we would like you to join the anti-H-Block party we established last year. We are actively recruiting women such as yourselves to run for office or make public appearances and speeches for us. That's why tomorrow would be a great start."

Maeve said, "That's a marvelous idea, absolutely. And Bridget, here, is just the one to do it."

"O dear God in heaven, no," said Bridget. "I could never do such a thing!"

"Of course ye can, my dear. Ye'r the very image of the Irish colleen, and ye've a lovely voice. No one wants to listen to an old crow like me."

"Ye'r no such thing, me dear friend," said Bridget.

She continued to try to protest, but Maeve raised her hand.

"Of course ye'll do it! Besides, as I said, it's ye'r man that's in H-Block."

"Then it's a deal," said Donnellon. "I'll pick you up at your hotel tomorrow at 10 a.m."

###

The press conference was scheduled for noon in front of Belfast's "Irish Republican Museum" at Conway Place. A platform had been erected there with two folding tables, four chairs, and microphones for Owen Carron, Bridget, Maeve, and Avery Donnellon. Reporters and television hookups from Ireland, Europe, and America were scattered in the crowd. Carron, a fifty-year-old ruddy-faced man with gray hair and beard, delivered a brief passionate speech highlighting the aims of his anti-H-Block movement. He then introduced, Donnellon, Maeve, and Bridget before turning the proceedings over to Bridget.

Bridget coughed nervously to clear her throat and fumbled with the microphone in front of her, causing the loudspeakers to crackle. She then shuffled the pages of her speech and began.

"Good day, ladies and gentlemen, and thank ye, Messrs. Carron and Donnellon for this opportunity to speak. Please bear with me, if ye will. I am new to all this." Bridget took a deep breath and smiled. Maeve winked at her. "We all know that the prisoners in H-Block have been the victims of brutal and inhuman treatment, but none of us knew, until recently, just how dreadful the treatment has been."

Over the next forty-five minutes, Bridget discussed the precipitating event: Margaret Thatcher's withdrawal of the "Special Status for Republican Prisoner," designating prisoners as common criminals rather than prisoners of war. As a result, Bridget explained, the prisoners had protested by refusing to wear prison garb. They went "on the blanket," living day and night in their cold, barren cells with nothing more than a blanket wrapped around their naked bodies.

Bridget described how the abuse escalated: how prisoners refused to leave their cells to shower or use the lavatory because brutal attacks by organized teams of prison guards awaited them, how they were then provided with nothing more than wash basins in their cells, how they were then refused even portable showers in their cells; how they refused to use the wash basins and smashed the meager furniture, how when the prisoners refused to leave their cells, the guards refused to clean the cells, how the "blanket protest" then deteriorated into "the dirty protest," during which prisoners were not able to empty their chamber pots, and protested by smearing their excrement on the walls of their cells.

"To this day"—Bridget raised her voice and went off script— "our H-Block men are living in these vile and disgusting conditions! What kind of bloody hellhole is this place? Where is the justice? In the name of God, what kind of people do this to other human beings? Again, where is the justice?" The audience broke into spontaneous, sustained applause, interrupting Bridget's remarks. She used this interlude to catch her breath before returning to her prepared remarks. She mentioned that guards were frequently drunk on duty, making them even more violent. She also indicted the medical staff for deliberately covering up the beatings. As for food? Bridget mentioned that the food was not only substandard and often rotten, it was also routinely contaminated by guards who added their urine and spit, as well as cockroaches and maggots.

As Bridget concluded her remarks, her voice began to shake.

"Not now, Bridget. Get on with it," counseled Maeve, squeezing her hand. Bridget gave her a grim smile and a firm nod and continued.

"We call on the people of Ireland and the nations of the world to condemn the British government and their governors in Belfast for their brutal and inhumane treatment of our husbands and brothers, our fathers and sons. The civilized world should know about and condemn those responsible for H-Block and its vicious crimes against humanity. It will be a forever stain, among the many other stains, on the reputation of what is left of the shrinking British Empire. However, for now, for this moment, we ask only that the government marshal the decency to provide these five basic human rights to the prisoners in H-Block: The right to wear civilian clothes; the right not to do prison work; the right of free association with other prisoners; access to educational and recreational pursuits; and the right to one visit, one letter, and one parcel per week."

Bridget stood, holding the microphone in her hand, and pleaded, "Isn't this the very least we can expect— that a government that claims to believe in human dignity, freedom, and justice live up to these principles and behave like a civilized people?" Bridget paused to catch her breath, then finished, "Thank you, ladies and gentlemen, for your consideration and patience." 115

There w as a m oment o f s ilence, b efore s cattered a pplause turned into robust cheers and a standing ovation. Flashing cameras captured the closing moments, while television reporters and cameramen quickly wrapped up their shoot and loaded their equipment into nearby vans in preparation for the evening news. Donnellon and Carron spent a few moments expressing their gratitude to Bridget and Maeve. They exchanged phone numbers, and Donnellon told them he would be maintaining close contact with them. Carron stated that this day was an important first step, and he looked forward to working with them. Once they departed, Maeve put her arm around Bridget's shoulder. "

Well done, me love. Now let's get our bags and get the hell out of here. I want to be home before the pubs close."

Chapter Thirty-Two

THE THREE ANCIENT WARRIORS GATHERED over seafood chowder and Guinness pints at Delaney's Pub and Eatery. Flynn wanted to have a serious discussion with Brian and Scully because he felt like they were wasting their time with the Provos in Armagh.

"Rather be castin' me line in Lough Neagh," he said.

Since they had boldly volunteered their services, Brian Connolly, Mike Scully, and Larry Flynn had been relegated to answering phones, running errands, and filing papers. They suspected that the "youngsters" viewed them as relics of a misty, Fenian past, little more than mascots, or worse yet, secretaries. Between spoonsful of cod and flounder lifted from their savory broth, they began an unfiltered assessment of their usefulness to this local IRA chapter. The trio suspected that they might, in fact, be of no operational value whatsoever to the younger generation of fighters. But since the chowder was delicious and they had no pressing plans for the day, they decided to brainstorm nonetheless to determine if they might not have something, anything, of value to contribute.

The singular item that galvanized all of them was prospect of a jailbreak. This, above all, quickened their pulses. Jailbreaking teased some of Brian's fondest recollections.

"Remember when we were lads with 'Billy' Pilkington and Sligo's Third West Division?" Brian asked.

"Oh yeah," said Flynn. "Those were some damn good days—attacks on the RIC barracks, train robberies, shooting 'Tans, stealing weapons, cash, and supplies. It was like the bleedin' Wild West."

"What I remember most," said Brian, "were the jailbreaks with Billy. Nothing scared old Billy Pilkington. He had the bollocks of a feckin rhinoceros. Remember, don't ye, Billy's escape from Dublin Castle? And that on the same Sunday Mick Collins's lads assassinated fourteen British spies, no less?"

Scully nodded. "I remember a few months later, when twenty of our fellas were being held in an old Mayo abbey by the local RIC. Wasn't it Billy himself who knocked on the abbey door to tell the guards to let our fellas free, or we would blow the feckin place to smithereens? He pointed to ten of us on foot and horseback, holding fiery torches and sticks of dynamite. Our lads were free in five minutes, and then we took the guards' weapons. And their boots."

Both old men nodded their heads, smiling.

"Ah sure, and I've become a sentimental old sod," said Brian, laughing. "But I've always had a soft spot in me heart for a good jailbreak."

"He could be a strange one, Billy could," said Scully. "One time, Jerry Mullaney—you remember him, small guy with a wild thatch of yellow hair, always smiling, but mean as a feckin python. Well, Billy took him and me on a train to snag and finish off two troublesome agents of the Crown. Well, we take these two 'blackguards,' as Billy called them—off the train, walk them down the road, and execute them. Then Billy says, 'Now get down on your knees and pray for them. They were your enemies. They are now your friends.' I never quite figured that one, praying for enemies we just killed. Gave me the chills, actually. Still does when I think of it."

"Well, we shouldn't be too surprised when we think of it," said Brian. "Didn't he, after the war, and after fighting with the Anti-Treaty boys, become a feckin Catholic priest? A missionary in Africa no less!"

The three went silent for a few moments. Brian and Flynn clouded the meeting with their cigarette smoke. Scully cracked the window to release it.

Brian rubbed his beard for a few moments, searching his memory. "Mullaney, Mullaney." Finally, he said, "Jerry Mullaney. I remember him. Always smiling. Always in for the joke like. After one skirmish, the two of us were drinkin' our pints in a Westport pub. For a little fella, he could drink, but it made him bold. And mean. That day, he taunted Paulie O'Rourke, a big hairy bastard from Clare. He staggered over to O'Rourke, looked up at him and said that he had heard from reliable sources that O'Rourke was the dumbest son-of-a-bitch in County Clare. O'Rourke told Mullaney to watch his filthy mouth. Mullaney laughed and then added that he had also heard that O'Rourke's wife was the ugliest woman in the county. 'Face like a trout,' the drunken Mullaney said. 'Or a flounder. Some kind of fuckin fish. I can't remember.'"

The men all laughed.

"Then he said, "The two of ye make quite a sorry feckin couple, don't ye?' With that, O'Rourke threw his massive, hairy arm around Mullaney's neck. He dragged him out of the pub, and with Mullaney gagging under his arm, he charged an old church wall across the road, intending to bash Mullaney's skull against it. And don't ye know, he failed to account for the fact that his head preceded Mullaney's? Sure enough, he smashes his own giant head against the wall at top speed and collapses in a bloody heap. Mullaney straightened up, shook his drunken body, and howled, 'I was right, was I not? He *is* the dumbest bastard in County Clare, maybe in all of Ireland!'"

Flynn and Scully laughed again, but Scully finally felt compelled to call the meeting to order.

"We're not getting any younger, lads. Let's get to our purpose and plan how we might best employ our experience and our skills if we are going to get involved in this escape plan."

Brian scoffed. "Skills?" He reminded his friends that all three of them were more than eighty years old and afflicted with some combination of knee, hip, neck, and back pain, bad hearing, failing eyesight, spotty memory, enlarged prostates, sketchy bowels, bladders, and unruly flatulence—any one of which, he suggested, would jeopardize the simplest mission. They grudgingly agreed but proceeded, nonetheless, on the off chance they might think of something. And in the final analysis, as they ordered another round, they acknowledged once again that they had nothing better to do.

Flynn began by touting his career as a tour bus driver. He knew the roads of the north and south intimately—the main roads; the hedge-bound, two-lane county roads; the little-known back roads; even the cattle trails. He tasked himself with assembling the maps, charting the roads that spider-webbed out from H-Block for fifty miles or more.

Scully had retired as a civil engineer and knew how to acquire aerial photographs, perhaps even photographs overlooking Maze Prison and the surrounding areas.

Brian spent his working days as a plumber with a small

construction firm, often working in tandem with electricians. His short, unhappy tenure at H-Block had afforded him a general impression of the interior layout of the prison. He told Scully that he would sketch what he thought might be weak spots from casual observation, but he said he would look for architectural drawings in Belfast's public records office as well to get a definitive picture of the floor plans, the location of junction boxes, guard-posting towers and stations, and the heights of fences. He also thought they should have someone working inside.

Flynn said they already had two or three prisoners working in the laundry, checking guards' schedules, even their level of attentiveness. He mentioned that the laundry and kitchen prisoners were also watching and timing the lorries that delivered supplies to the prison, trying to decide how and if they could be used in the escape.

They agreed to have their research completed in a week's time.

During the war of independence, Flynn's puckish manner had marked him early on as an untrustworthy warrior—a soldier who would either retreat at the rumor of gunfire or be killed in his first encounter because he refused to take seriously the "mortal" part of mortal combat. Members of his platoon predicted that he would, at some inappropriate moment, be howling so loud at one of his own jokes that he would reveal his squad's position, whereupon they would all be machine-gunned or mortared to death. Not surprisingly, he early on found himself isolated from his comrades when the shooting started.

What his detractors failed to account for, at the time, was that for all of Flynn's goofy gregariousness, he had an exceedingly violent temper.

In one early encounter in the hills of Roscommon, Flynn's squad was surrounded and outnumbered by a platoon of British soldiers. In addition to his rifle, Flynn ostentatiously carried two holstered German-made Luger PO8 pistols with two bandoliers of bullets crisscrossing his chest in the manner of Poncho Villa. During this firefight, an enemy bullet grazed his face and detached his left earlobe.

Flynn flew immediately into an insane rage. He abandoned his crouching cover behind a large oak, dropped his rifle, and charged the enemy tree line with his two guns blazing. And although he took a bullet in the shoulder and a glancing shot on his thigh, he killed or wounded enough of the enemy to unnerve them and chase them from their positions. His berserk maneuver opened a path for him and his platoon to escape. Scully later joked that the enemy were more upset by Flynn's foul temper than by his marksmanship.

While this unpredictable attitude served Flynn well in combat, it cost him one well-paying job as a tour bus driver. Transporting a bus full of wealthy Germans along a narrow road in Connemara one summer, Flynn's bus was blocked by a farmer moving thirty or so cows from one pasture to another. The sluggish movement of the herd made Flynn apoplectic.

He honked his horn repeatedly, but the farmer ignored him. Then he moved his bus precariously close to the cows, threatening to run them down. When he opened his bus door and told the farmer to get his cattle the hell off the road, the farmer told Flynn to go fuck himself—which Flynn hated. Furious, he stopped the bus, opened the door, and engaged the farmer in a lengthy fist fight, a fight that had to be broken up by the local Gardai. Flynn was taken to the local courthouse, where he paid a fine for disorderly conduct. When the bus returned to Galway, the Germans complained to Flynn's boss. Flynn was summarily fired and went on the dole for six months.

Chapter Thirty-Three

MARY AND TIM WANDERED THE AISLES in Macy's men's department, looking for bargains during their "March Madness Sale." They picked out three white shirts, three blue ties (two striped and one solid), and a pair of comfortable shoes.

Tim also tried on a green plaid sports jacket, glancing at himself in the mirror. He checked the price tag on his sleeve and raised his eyebrows. Mary studied him while he turned around.

"No. Not that one. Try this one." Mary handed him a blue blazer.

Tim tried it on. "How's this?" he asked.

"It's better," Mary said. "But still . . . " She stroked her chin as she looked at Tim. "I have a better idea," she said. "Let's go."

They left a stack of jackets and slacks on the display table but took the shirts, ties, and shoes to the cash register.

When they got back to the apartment, Mary laid out three of Marty's old suits on Tim's bed. She held a jacket up to him. "These just might fit. Marty hardly ever wore them, so they still look new." She picked up the pants and held them next to Tim. "Might have to take these in a little . . . here. . . but try on this jacket."

It fit well enough.

"Perfect," said Mary. She stood back and admired him. "Ye'r date will be a happy lass when she sees how handsome ye are!"

Tim shook his head. "Sure, it's not really a date, ye know, Aunt Mary. She's just a friend like."

"Whatever ye say, Tim," said Mary. "Ye look grand all the same." She opened her arms to Tim. Tim beamed and, for the first time, he hugged her. She laughed heartily as she embraced him and patted his back. "Me fine young man. We'll take care of ye."

Chapter Thirty-Four

IN HIS DINGY CELL, ILLUMINATED by a single bare light bulb, Terence lay on his rancid cot, reading Tim's smuggled letter, his diminished naked body wrapped in a stained and foul-smelling gray blanket. His ribs and jaw ached from the beating administered the day before by Hennessy, the worst of the "screws" on their block. Hennessy was an obese, drunken sadist who wantonly attacked prisoners on a random basis. Yesterday was Terence's toss of the dice. Seemingly out of nowhere, Hennessy opened his cell and started kicking and punching him.

Now, with Tim's letter in his hands, Terence felt even worse. After twice starting to read it, he put it down briefly to wipe his face before picking it up again. When he finished, he pulled the cover over his head, curled into a fetal position, and wailed.

Several hours later, he settled into the corner of his cell to write Tim. Near him, taped to the wall, was an unframed photo of Terence with his wife and son. He retrieved his hidden pen and paper, paused to wipe the dried froth from his lips, and started to write. Curses and shouts echoed down the hall as a guard strutted by, twirling his baton.

Dear Timmy, I read your letter today, and it broke my heart. There is nothing in the world I want more than to be home with you and your Ma. But we are engaged in a kind of combat here in H-Block—a battle of wills. The guards are bewildered by our willingness to stand up to their blows; and because they do not understand us, they fear us. Our own Terence MacSwiney once said: 'It is not those who can inflict the most but those who can endure the most who will conquer.' My dear Tim, I hope our protests work and we are free again soon. But, if that does not happen, you should know that they did not break me. They did not, and will not, break any of us, and we will win, we will conquer. Your understanding will fortify and inspire me in this battle. In this, you will be my partner. Be kind to your Ma, your Aunt Mary, and Uncle Gary. And do well in school. Your loving Da

Terence rolled up his letter and hid it under his mattress till it could be smuggled out. Then he lay down to rest.

A prisoner from a nearby cell, alarmed by Terence's daylong silence, called to him.

"Connolly! Connolly! Are ye with us, lad? Speak up. Speak up, lad!"

In his solitary cell, Terence felt too exhausted to speak. The alarmed prisoner, Pat McCahill, a Provo from Glenties, Donegal, shouted through his door slot and banged his tin cup on the door, shouting, "Guard! Guard! Hennessy, get yer fat useless arse in here!"

Chapter Thirty-Five

AS THE HIGH SCHOOL BAND PLAYED familiar ballads, dim light filtered through the gym's rafters, which were decorated with green and red Japanese lanterns and multicolored streamers. A poster at the entrance announced, "The April in Paris Senior Ball." Couples shuffled around the crowded dance floor. Others gathered on the perimeter, talking, laughing. Cooper, Benson, and Blake, decked out in jackets and ties, stood with their dates several yards from the entrance to the gym, passing back and forth a fifth of whiskey in a paper bag. Tim and Gina passed them as they made their entrance. Tim looked uncomfortable wearing his late cousin's unfashionable suit, which featured outsize shoulder pads. Gina also looked uncomfortable in her flouncy, pink, low-cut satin dress, which dramatically highlighted her muscular body and large breasts. Wobbling precariously in her high heels, she stood five inches taller than Tim.

When Cooper saw them, he howled and hooted in drunken glee.

"Oh, Jesus. This is rich! This looks like something out of a fuckin Tarzan movie!" He proceeded to make mock kissing sounds in the direction of Tim and Gina, grinding his hips lasciviously. "Hi, lovers!" he said.

Benson chimed in, "Hi Va-Gina!" Benson's date slapped him on the shoulder, though she laughed. Tim, no longer intimidated by this trio, started angrily toward them, but Gina pulled him away.

127

"Fuck them, Tim. They're just a bunch of morons."

Tim briefly stared at Blake, causing him to look away.

Cooper noticed the exchange.

"Ooooh . . . what was that bad look about, Blake? Backin' down from the Donkey Boy?"

Blake blustered, "Nothing. Just some bullshit."

Gina grabbed Tim's arm and pulled him over to the table with a punch bowl. Tim poured a couple of drinks into paper cups and handed one to her. The band began a slow, slightly off-key version of "The Wonder of You."

"Let's drink these later," Gina said. "I wanna dance."

Tim hesitated.

"What's wrong? You're not embarrassed, are you?"

"No. No," he stammered. "Just that . . . I, uh, don't know how to dance. I mean . . . I can do a jig or a reel, but not this." He shrugged.

"Shit. Ain't nothin to it," she said. "Here, put your arms around me, and we'll just shuffle around." As they moved around the floor, Tim gradually got the hang of it. He especially liked the feel of Gina's large breasts pressed against his neck.

When the fast music began, they stayed on the floor. Gina moved well and rhythmically.

Tim stumbled with his steps. Cooper and Benson staggered over to where they were dancing, intent on trouble.

Cooper gestured with a whiskey bottle in his hand.

"Have you ever seen a more ridiculous sight in your life than this pasty-faced fuckin' bog trotter dancing with Miss Queen Kong?"

Tim's body stiffened. "Fuck off, you drunken wanker."

"Oh, a 'wanker,' am I?" Cooper replied. "Well, I sure as shit don't know what a 'wanker' is, but I sure know a skinny faggot and a burly dyke when I see one."

Tim lunged toward him, but Gina restrained him.

Cooper wiggled and pretended to be frightened. "Ooooo . . . how very scary!" His date giggled.

"Tim, this slack-jawed bedwetter ain't worth the effort," Gina said. "And besides, violence never solves anything."

She walked slowly toward Cooper and said, "Ain't that right, Cooper?"

Just as he nodded and grinned stupidly at her, she hit him square in the face with a roundhouse, closed-fist haymaker, knocking him flat on the floor.

He was out cold. Blood spouted from his nose like an open spigot. Cooper's date screamed.

"Except maybe once in a while. Eh? Mr. Cooper?" Leaning over him, she said, "What's that? Cat got your tongue?"

"Jaysus H. Christ!" said Tim, astonished.

"Holy shit!" said Benson, staggering backwards.

Cooper's date placed her hands on her face, shrieking uncontrollably.

Gina laughed heartily. She opened and closed her fist, adjusted her dress, and hoisted her breasts. As a crowd gathered near the flattened Cooper, Gina grabbed Tim's arm.

"Let's get the hell out of here."

Together, they stepped over Cooper's supine, unconscious body, blood dripping from his flattened nose. On the way out of the gym, Tim scowled once again at Blake, but he looked away.

The band played on, but the music faded behind Tim and Gina as they left the gym.

"Let's walk around the track," Tim said.

"Sure. First, let me take off these goddam shoes." She placed her left hand on his shoulder and removed them. "Whoa, Bessie!" she said. "That's better."

Tim burst into laughter.

"Jaysus, Gina. that was some bloody shot ye landed! Almost ripped his drunken head off his shoulders." Gina lifted her right arm and flexed her bicep.

"That fool's lucky I didn't hit him as hard as I could have."

"Where'd ye learn to punch like that?"

"Older brother loved to box with me," she said.

"Brother? What's he doin' now?" Tim asked.

"He's dead. He and my mother were killed in a car crash two years ago."

"I'm sorry, Gina. That's awful," said Tim.

"Thanks," she said. "Sometimes it seems like it happened fifteen years ago; sometimes it seems like last week." She turned away, lowering her voice and her eyes. "Not for my father, though," she sighed. "He still talks about them all the time, like they're still alive. Sometimes, I hear him talking *to* my mom. He thinks I don't hear him."

Tim murmured, "Like me great-grandfather and his son—the grandfather I never knew. Sure, some wounds go so deep, they never heal. But he's a good Da, is he?"

"Yeah. The best," she said. "He used to work his ass off. Never complained, except if I didn't do good in school. But now he can't work, and he don't know where he is half the time. So . . . " Gina opened her arms to the sky and swung in a circle, sighing deeply, then changing the subject. "What about your folks?"

"Me mother's runnin' our small farm in Sligo and workin' at the local fish market. Me Da's . . . " Tim went silent.

"What?" Gina asked.

"In prison," said Tim. "He's in prison, one of the hunger strikers."

She shook her head. "Geez, Tim. I had no idea." She put her hand on his shoulder.

"He . . . " Tim started to explain, but then he stopped. Gina tousled his hair and embraced him.

"A pair of lost souls, ain't we? Strange . . . We're from two different worlds, greenhorn. But somehow we're a lot alike."

"Yes, I guess we are," said Tim. "And ye . . . ye have become me best friend. Me only friend, actually." The comment unexpectedly unsettled Gina. She cleared her throat, regrouped, and changed the subject.

"Geez, Tim. All this sorrowful shit is wearin' me out. Whatta ya say we call it a night? We both got tough workouts tomorrow. State Championships next week." Gina then assumed a playful formality. "So, how about you take me home, Mr. Connolly?"

Tim tried to rally in kind. "Me pleasure, Miss Carboney."

"That's Car*bone*, you jagoff. Christ, you really are thick." As they walked off the track, Tim clumsily put his right arm around Gina's waist. She put her left arm around his neck, dangling her high heels from her right hand.

Chapter Thirty-Six

MCCAHILL NIBBLED ON A HANGNAIL and slumped on his bed. Then he retreated into an agitated silence as the guard's thumping boots echoed in the corridor.

When the guard arrived at Terence's cell, he peered through the door slot and saw Terence spread out on his mattress—weak, motionless, and glassy-eyed, but still alive. He unlocked Terence's cell, walked over to him, and felt his forehead.

"How're ye doin, lad?" he asked while placing his hand on Terence's forehead. "Ye've a bit of a temperature. I'd help ye if I could, but I can't do much while ye'r strikin'." Terence blinked at him and twitched his head. McCahill heard the guard's voice and shouted.

"Who are ye, Mister? You ain't Hennessy. Where's that prick?"

"Me name's McQuarrie. Doug McQuarrie. So, ye'r right, inmate. I ain't Hennessy."

"He transfer? Quit? Was he fired?" asked McCahill. "That dirty bastard."

"Well, yer Mr. Hennessy has done none of those. But for sure he won't be back," said McQuarrie. "He's recently joined the choir of angels. Or some feckin choir, I'm not sure which one."

"Dead?" asked McCahill.

"As a fuckin' doorknob," said McQuarrie. "One of your IRA boyos put a bullet in the back of his fat head last night. Sayonara! Arrivederci! Bon Voyage!"

"That's wonderful news. Ye don't seem too broken up, Doug," said McCahill.

"Good riddance, I say. Nobody here liked him. He was a drunken fool and a sadistic arsehole," he said. "This is nasty work, as ye know, inmate, and sometimes we have to knock heads. But he went too far. He really enjoyed hurting people, breaking the bones, like, ye know?"

"Yeah, Doug, sure I know. Well, I'm glad ye'r here. Me buddy there is in bad shape, so I hope ye can keep an eye on him from time to time," said McCahill.

"I'll do what I can," said McQuarrie as he shut Terence's door and returned to his post.

McCahill, in a gravelly whisper, said, "Connolly, Connolly . . . can you hear me, lad?"

Tim responded, his voice weak. "Yeah, Pat."

"Connolly," McCahill said, "Give up this protest. Start eating—we got somethin goin'. He mentioned something about a planned escape, but Terence was silent.

"Think about it."

Terence did think about it. After rereading Tim's letter, he slept for several hours. When he woke up, he decided to start eating again.

Pat McCahill had taken a circuitous route to H-Block. He was a defrocked priest, but not for his long-term dalliances with two widows and a wealthy spinster from his parish in Glenveigh. He confessed those sins weekly to his monsignor, pledging never to repeat them, and he was always forgiven. But Father McCahill had developed expensive tastes that could not be satisfied on his meager stipend. He lusted not only for these parish women, but also for fine wine and cozy weekends in posh Killarney hotels. So, he started skimming the Sunday collections. The amount of skimming increased with McCahill's appetites. Eventually, he dipped his craven hands into the parish collection till one time too often and was snared by the bishop's accountant.

In McCahill's parish, womanizing and heavy drinking were forgivable mortal sins in the eyes of Holy Mother the Church, but till pilfering teased the outer limits of redemption. McCahill's unceremonious banishment from the priesthood left a vacuum in his desire to be of service. However misguided, this desire propelled him into the open arms of the IRA, where he found a new vocation in munitions, sending souls to heaven not with prayers but with Semtex.

Chapter Thirty-Seven

TRACK FANS, COMPETITORS, FAMILY, FRIENDS, and media descended on Randall's Island, filling the stadium to near capacity. The NY State High School Track and Field Championship was the major sporting event on the April calendar.

Tim was the sole runner from St. Jude's to qualify for the eight-hundred-meter final. Calm, confident, and focused, he took his place in the second lane. As he leaned forward on the starting line, the starter raised his pistol, set the runners, and then fired.

At the first turn, Tim settled comfortably into second place. By the two-hundred-meter mark, the first-place runner and Tim separated from the field. Tim continued to draft off the right shoulder of the leader as they moved toward the far turn. The bell rang four times as they completed the first lap.

Twenty-three seconds later, at the six-hundred-meter mark, Tim bolted to the lead. The crowd stood to their feet and roared with encouragement. Arms pumping, face wreathed in fury, Tim stormed up the final straightaway, breaking the tape fifty meters ahead of the now-second-place runner. He slowed to a trot with his arms in the air, breathing heavily.

Quigley clicked his stopwatch and leapt in the air.

He shouted to Tim. "You did it, son."

Tim, bent over, breathing heavily, said, "Did what, Coach?"

"You hit 1:46:07! Tim . . . you broke the state record!"

His teammates swarmed over him, mussing his hair, shaking

his hand, and patting him on the back. Blake waited until everyone else had finished, then offered his hand. Tim took it.

"Good race, man," said Blake. "Congratulations. You deserve it."

Tim looked suspiciously into his eyes for a few seconds, then said, "Thanks."

Cooper watched the celebration from a distance, scowling behind his bandaged nose and black eyes. Gina just brushed by him and joined the well-wishers. She threw her arms around a laughing Tim, lifted him in the air, and swung him around. The coach joined his team, quietly congratulating Tim and telling him how proud he was.

As he walked away from his team's celebration, Quigley experienced a wave of sadness. He turned and watched as Tim, Gina, and their teammates walked off the track. He checked his watch, packed his briefcase, and headed home.

When he arrived at his apartment, he tossed his jacket and briefcase on the sofa, went to the cupboard for a tumbler, filled it with ice, then covered the ice with his Johnny Walker Red. He turned on the local news and waited five minutes for the sports segment. He raised the volume when toothy news anchor Jerry Douglas turned to his smiling female partner, blond-haired, long-legged former beauty queen, Tiffany Morneau.

"Well, Tiffany, I understand we have some big news on the local sports scene."

"That's right, Jerry," she said. "And here with that story and the rest of the sports highlights is Chip Mullins . . . Chip?" The camera turned to crew-cutted Chip Mullins, all smiles and bouncing a sheaf of papers in his hands.

"That's right, Jerry and Tiffany, big news indeed," he said. "At the New York State Track and Field Championships today, Tim Connolly, the young Irishman they're calling 'The Boy from Mullaghmore,' obliterated the state record for the eight hundred meters, a record coincidentally set by his coach, John Quigley, thirty-five years ago . . ."

Quigley held the TV knob for an uncertain moment, then switched it off before Chip could show a replay of the race. He poured himself another drink and sat on his couch, staring into his glass. After a few minutes, he rose and retrieved an old Bell and Howell 8mm projector and two film canisters from his closet. He spooled a reel that he removed from a liver-spotted canister, then turned the projector toward a blank wall.

The wall suddenly came alive with speckled black-and-white footage of triumphant races from Quigley's athletic prime. He withdrew into another time and place as he listened to the voice from the projector:

"John Quigley, America's top middle-distance runner and an almost sure bet for Olympic Gold, takes the lead at the bell lap and never gives it up. He wins the race by more than thirty meters over a world-class field."

When the race highlights from the first reel were finished, Quigley spooled the reel from the second canister and played another hour of triumphant footage from the early fifties. When this one finished, its constant flapping roused him from a half sleep. He put his left hand on his forehead, then shook the empty whiskey glass in his right. After turning off the projector, he staggered to the kitchen and poured another drink. Returning to the living room, he glanced at the pictures of his wife and took a seat next to the phone. He stared at the crumpled letter from her attorney, squatting like an avenging imp on his coffee table, then picked it up and threw it across the room. After pausing for a few minutes, he picked up the receiver, took a deep breath, and dialed. When the other party answered, he cleared his throat and attempted to sound sober, buoyant, upbeat.

"Linda? he asked.

"John?"

"Yes, hon. I hope I'm not . . . "

"You know you're not supposed to call," she said.

"Yeah . . . I know . . . but I was just thinking of you and the kids and wanted to see how everything . . . "

"We're all fine, John," she said curtly.

"I'm glad . . . Yeah. That's great."

"I can't talk long, John. I have an appointment with my counselor. But things seem to be going well for you with your team. You have quite a special runner, don't you?"

"Yeah . . . things are going well at school. And Tim Connolly? Yeah, he's quite a young man . . . Listen, I . . . uh . . . was hoping we could catch dinner soon. We need to talk."

"John, we've been over all this. I can't do this anymore."

Yeah. . . Okay . . . No problem . . . Sure . . . Well, send my love to the kids. And I . . ."

The clicking sound interrupted Quigley's "miss you."

Distraught, he rubbed his face with his left hand and smashed his glass on the table with his right hand. Ice and whiskey flew up as the glass shattered. Blood dripped from the gash in his hand. He picked out some pieces of glass, then clenched it and wept.

Chapter Thirty-Eight

TIM SAT ACROSS FROM HIS COACH. Quigley massaged his tired face and bloodshot eyes with one hand. His other was heavily bandaged and hidden from Tim's sight. "I'm glad you came in this morning, Tim. That was a remarkable race yesterday, young man."

"Thanks, Coach. I felt great. Ye know—" Tim paused. "I couldn't have done it without ye."

"Thanks for that, Tim." He lowered his head, smiled a sad smile, and nodded. "Is there anything special you need today?"

"Not really, Coach," said Tim. "I just wanted to tell you I might be late for practice today." He looked at the clock on the wall. "I have to go. Me aunt and uncle are meeting me at church. The priest is saying a special Mass for me Da."

"I'll drive you and join you, if you don't mind," Quigley offered. "I haven't been to church in a long while. It'll do me some good—and certainly confuse the hell out of the devil."

"Grand. Yeah. Thanks, Coach," said Tim.

"I'll meet you by the flagpole in five minutes."

After Tim left his office, Quigley grabbed his jacket and briefcase. Before leaving, however, he knocked on Brother Frank's office door. The door was partially open, so Quigley entered the empty office. Moments later, the brother, distracted and disheveled, emerged from the locker room.

Quigley said, "I'm going to a Special Mass for Tim Connolly's father. I'll be back in two hours."

Brother Frank gave him a strange look but said nothing.

As Quigley was about to leave, he caught a glimpse of Blake in the locker room archway and stopped. Blake's face was bruised, his lip and right eye swollen, and his nose bleeding. Quigley went to him.

"Tyrone, what happened?" Blake turned away from him and retreated from the doorsill.

Brother Frank intervened. "This is no concern of yours, Mr. Quigley. This is strictly a disciplinary matter. You best be on your way."

"No concern?" said Quigley. "For Christ's sake, Frank, he's just a boy, and he's one of my runners! What kind of shop do you run here anyway? Do you just batter students every day for the hell of it?"

Brother Frank stood close to Quigley and spoke in a tense whisper. "I told you to leave. I warned you once before . . . " Then his tone changed. "Do I smell whiskey on your breath, Mr. Quigley? That's interesting. Another strike against you. If you value your job, you'll disappear right now."

Quigley felt trapped. He glanced grimly in the direction of Blake, who had retreated into the locker room. Then, looking contemptuously at Brother Frank, he shook his head.

"Unbelievable," he said, and left.

Chapter Thirty-Nine

QUIGLEY DROPPED TIM AT THE ENTRANCE of Resurrection Church and parked his car. He'd been bitterly silent on the way to the church, seething with anger after his encounter with Brother Frank, thinking perhaps he should have had it out with him then and there, but he was worried that it might get him fired.

Inside the church, statues were covered by purple satin cloth. It would be another week before Easter Sunday tradition allowed their removal. Tim joined his aunt and uncle in a front-row pew and stood as Mass began. A few minutes later, Quigley limped down the main aisle, spotted Tim and his family, genuflected, and filed into their aisle. Quigley shook hands with Gary and Mary.

Attendance for this morning Mass was sparse, populated mostly by gray-haired women bundled in woolen, gray overcoats and a few retired men anxious to be out of the house, fill an idle hour, and be seen by their neighbors.

After the opening prayers, the priest ascended the pulpit, read the gospel, and delivered a blissfully anodyne homily. He then briefly, very briefly, mentioned the special petition for Tim's father and offered a terse promise of prayers for his physical and spiritual well-being. He did not, however, mention the torture, the hunger strikes, or the human rights abuses inflicted on Terence Connolly and sanctioned by the British government.

Tim bristled and whispered audibly, "That's it? That's it? We came here for that?" Impulsively, he stood and shouted. "That's it, Father? Ye'r not going to say anything about me Da being tortured by the bloody Brits? He's an innocent man for Christ's sake, Father! He never hurt anyone, and he's dyin' now! What about the bloody injustice? What about the injustice?"

Shaken by this breach of church decorum, the priest descended the pulpit, walked slowly to the altar rail, and spoke quietly but firmly to Tim. He nodded his head as he spoke, his hands clasped to his chest in a studiously pious manner. He told Tim that his father was in God's hands and that he and his parishioners would be praying for him.

Tim glowered at him and shook his head. "This is bloody pathetic, Father. Pathetic." Scattered murmurs echoed behind him.

An angry old woman in the rear of the church shouted, "Sit down, young man."

An old man counseled, "Behave yourself, kid, you're in God's house." The congregation buzzed with surprise and confusion. Mary took Tim's hand and gently tried to pull him back in his seat. The boy resisted. Instead, he left the pew, storming up the aisle and out of the church. Mary then rose to Tim's defense.

"He's right, ye know, Father. Crimes are being committed against innocent people in Belfast. Catholics especially are being persecuted. Don't ye have some sort of pastoral duty to defend them and condemn their persecutors?"

The priest struggled to maintain his ministerial composure. He stated that it was not the Church's job to get embroiled in partisan political controversies, but rather to minister to the spiritual well-being of people of all nationalities and political leanings.

"Many of our parishioners are British or have family or

business connections in the United Kingdom," he said. "The Church cannot get in the middle of the latest political controversies that may divide our worshippers."

Gary had been growing increasingly restive during this conversation, and he finally stood, his voice trembling.

"This Diocese, this Church, and you . . . you, in particular, Father Nagle, had no trouble with political controversy when you and this whole diocese justified the Vietnam war and told us that we had a moral and patriotic duty to fight against the Communists—even in the face of the politicians' lies, lies that caused the senseless deaths of hundreds of thousands of innocent people, including fifty-seven thousand American soldiers. Including . . . including my own sweet son."

Parishioners were now grumbling louder and talking among themselves. Gary caught his breath and pointed directly at the priest. "And you stand here now, and you tell us that you cannot condemn the vile injustice being inflicted on a single innocent man by a corrupt government—a relative of one of your parishioners, and a devout Catholic man at that! Tell me, please, what good are you and your lame prayers? Really, what damn good? All your pious mumbo-jumbo . . . I—I, for one, don't know how I have put up with it for so long, but no more . . . I'll be goddamned if I ever set foot back in this church, or any church again."

With that, a shaken Gary and Mary stalked up the aisle and out of the church to a mixture of boos and applause. Quigley, stunned by what he just witnessed, followed them.

As the red-faced priest returned to the altar, he gestured angrily to the organist to play. She immediately pounded the keys as though the sheer volume of her groaning instrument might exorcise this infernal moment from the memory of the congregation and the church itself.

Tim was waiting and pacing outside the church. He started to speak when he saw them.

"I'm sorry, I didn't mean to . . ." Gary and Mary walked silently to Tim and embraced him before he could finish his apology.

"No, Tim. Thank you. Thank you for speaking out," said Gary. Mary kissed him on the cheek.

The coach watched them for a moment before he spoke.

"That was truly the most exciting Mass I've ever been to. Unbelievable. I can't begin to tell you what a strange day this has been so far, and it's not even noon yet!" Quigley then changed his tone. "This was unfortunate. What happened to all of you today just makes a bad situation worse. I'm sorry. I know this has been a tough time for all of you, but . . ." He turned to Mary and Gary. "I'm going to tell you what you already know. This is a fine young man you have here."

Surprised and embarrassed, Tim offered a quiet, "Thank ye."

"We appreciate you telling us that, Mr. Quigley," said Mary. "And we appreciate the care ye've shown him."

"Honestly, Mrs. Laherty, he's been an inspiration to me."

Changing the subject, Gary asked Quigley, "What can you tell us about this Brother Frank? I don't remember him being there when Marty was a student."

Quigley shook his head. "Not much. He pretty much keeps to himself. He seems to run the place, though, and he runs it like a tyrant and a bully. He seems to enjoy humiliating and beating students. He's a mean bastard . . . pardon my French, ma'am. He has a real mean streak."

Tim angrily echoed these words. "That's for damn sure."

Mary was surprised by her nephew's tone.

"Do ye know anything else about him, Tim, other than what he did to ye?"

Tim replied cryptically, "No, m'am . . . well, yes, but nothin I can talk about right now." Gary looked quizzically at Quigley, and both men looked at Tim.

Quigley registered concern, but he dropped the subject for the moment. "Well, on a brighter note, we've got the AAU Open Championships starting in late June, just after graduation. That is our target. Two weeks of trial races—district trials, then regionals, in order to qualify for the finals in July. This is the biggest race of the year," said Quigley. "We're aiming for Tim to qualify in the eight hundred meters. It won't be easy. He'll be competing against older athletes, the best middle-distance runners in America, but it should be exciting. So, we have a lot to look forward to.

Tim nodded his agreement, then noticed Quigley's bandaged hand.

"What happened to your hand, Coach?"

Quigley looked at it, a painful reminder of the previous night's turmoil. "Cut it on a piece of glass. Just careless."

Chapter Forty

BRIAN AND FLYNN SAT ACROSS from Scully at the kitchen table in Flynn's sparsely furnished one-bedroom flat. Flynn's mangy, mud-spattered dog slept in the corner on a filthy pillow, intermittently snoring and whimpering. Smoke from Flynn's cigarette floated in curling sheets above their heads. Each man sipped his cup of tea and looked at his notes as he prepared to discuss what he'd found.

Scully went first. He stood between them, unfolding an aerial photo of the prison and laying it on the table.

"This is interesting," Brian commented, "because I'm not sure that a single inmate has the slightest idea what the overall layout of the prison looks like. With so many places within places, you can see why they call it 'Maze.'"

"Finding this photo was ridiculously easy," Scully said. "It was front page in the *Daily Mail* two years ago. Hard to imagine anyone running this operation hadn't seen it. It shows the main gate, side entrances, and exits—we should be able to calculate distances with a slide rule."

Next, Flynn moved the teacups to the perimeter of the table and produced a map on which he had circled the streets and roads around the prison, spreading out for more than thirty kilometers in all directions. He'd color-coded the roads with highlighter: the main routes in yellow, the secondary in blue, the country roads in red, and the farm paths in green. He also indicated the paths off the main roads leading into the wooded and forested areas. These areas would provide cover, especially the first few nights, when the armored vehicles and helicopters would be flooding the immediate areas with high-powered searchlights.

Brian produced a few details from his brief time at H-Block. He remembered the approximate width and length of the hallways. He also remembered that the center of operations for each block was located at the horizontal line at the center of the "H" connecting the two vertical lines of cells. He indicated those on the photo.

Given the layout of Maze, he assessed that an escape from all the prison blocks simultaneously was unlikely. A plan could only work for one, or at most two blocks. He made notes of junction boxes, boilers, plumbing lines, and exterior and interior power lines. Brian calculated that his information was not as accurate or as valuable as that supplied by Scully and Flynn, but they would offer it nevertheless to the lads planning the escape. He told them that he'd tried to secure the exact architectural drawings from the public records office in Belfast, but the archivist was instantly suspicious and refused his request. When Brian persisted, the archivist picked up the phone.

"Damned if I didn't hop the hell out of there in a feckin heartbeat when he picked up that phone." Brian chuckled. "In hindsight, I don't think I made a favorable first impression—what with the bushy beard, the shabby clothes, and the scar. And maybe the crutch. Certainly the bleedin' crutch! I probably reminded him of Long John Silver . . . without the eye patch and the feckin parrot."

They handed over their results to the escape planners at the

Armagh headquarters later that day. Jerry Finlay, the head of local operations, thanked them for their effort. Though much of it duplicated what they already had, he said some of it was new and would be extremely useful—the coded maps especially. He told Brian not to worry about the architectural drawings, since they already had them. He mentioned that escape plans were proceeding at a fast pace, and they were coordinating almost daily with a small team of H-7 inmates.

"The most delicate part of the plan right now," said Finlay, "will be smuggling the latest information and the necessary weapons into their hands. Once they set the date and time, we will have our men on site when the lads make their break." He told Brian, Scully, and Flynn that he would certainly keep them in mind if he had some meaningful way to employ them.

Chapter Forty-One

AFTER CLEANING AND REBANDAGING his right hand over the bathroom sink, Quigley looked around his apartment, taking inventory. Things had to change. He stared at the mess—the empty whiskey bottle, the chunks and splinters of glass scattered on the table and floor from the previous night. He took in the mantle's tarnished trophies and faded photos, ghosts of glories past. The crumpled letter from Linda's attorney stared back at him from the corner of the room. Once he finished scanning it all, he walked into the bathroom, ran a washcloth under the cold water, then pressed it to his face. As he dried off, he contemplated the weariness in his eyes—the red veins a roadmap charting his journey to this dead end.

Then he moved. In the kitchen pantry he collected a broom, a dustpan, and a large cardboard box. He swept up the broken glass and threw it and the empty whiskey bottle in the trash. In the cupboard, he grabbed two unopened bottles of Johnnie Walker Red, poured the fragrant amber potion down the sink, and dropped the bottles in the trash. Then he filled the cardboard box with his trophies, his medals and ribbons, his faded sports photos, and his liver-spotted cans of 8MM film. He hauled the trash and the box of memorabilia down the back stairs to the yard behind the apartment building, where he tossed the box and the trash into the dumpster and went back upstairs. Then Quigley took a deep breath, unfolded the crumpled letter, and called Linda.

When she didn't answer, he left a long message on her machine.

Chapter Forty-Two

BROTHER FRANK TOOK A SEAT in the bleachers of the empty gym just before the 11 a.m. class arrived. He sat sipping coffee from a paper cup. Minutes later, an animated Quigley arrived and blew his whistle.

"Okay, gentlemen, fall into formation." Quigley noticed the brother glaring at him but ignored his presence. As Quigley called his students to their exercises, Frank finished his coffee, crumpled his cup, and exited the gym.

He went directly to the principal's office.

Father Kenney was pulling files from his cabinet when Brother Frank walked in unannounced.

"Good morning, Frank. How are you today?" he inquired.

Brother Frank skirted the usual pleasantries. "This Quigley character must go, Jim. I'm telling you, this guy is totally unfit to teach students. I've checked into his last two jobs. He was fired from both. They wouldn't say why, but now I know."

His vehemence unnerved Father Kenney. "What's brought this on, Frank? He seems to be doing a great job for us."

"Jim, he's a drunk. Every morning he reeks of whiskey. He's a disgrace."

Father Kenney replied, "This is really quite sudden, Frank. I'll need to investigate this. I can't just fire a man without all the facts."

"What's to think about, Jim?" said Brother Frank. "I know a rotten apple when I see one. We've got a responsibility to our kids.

They need a strong hand to guide them, not some damn boozer. What if the parents learn about him, or our alumni, or the diocese?"

Father Kenney retreated behind his desk. "I don't know," he waffled. "But . . . well, I'll talk to him. You may be right, Frank. Yes," he said weakly, "I'll call him in."

"I think that's best, Jim."

Chapter Forty-Three

THE ST. JUDE RUNNERS WERE JOGGING on the track and stretching on the infield, waiting for the coach. Quigley soon arrived and made his way to the starting line, taking his time. He called the team together on the infield.

"Gentleman, this is a sad day for me." He pulled out a handkerchief and wiped it across his nose. "Earlier today, I was asked to tender my resignation. I was fired."

Team members stirred and murmured.

Tim shouted, "No! No!" Cooper shook his fist, smiled, and glanced at Blake and Benson. Blake turned away. Quigley raised his arm in a halting gesture.

"I'll spare you the details. Suffice it to say, not everyone thought I was doing a good enough job."

Tim glared at Cooper and approached him. "You're behind this, aren't ye? Bastard!"

Cooper smirked and shoved him away. "Eat shit, donkey."

Tim charged Cooper and knocked him to the ground. The rest of the team gathered around them. Quigley jumped in and pulled Tim off.

"Break it up. Everybody else, scatter," he shouted.

Gina noticed the ruckus from the shot-put area and came running to the infield. Meanwhile, Cooper stood in a daze and delicately touched his already damaged nose while Benson dutifully attended to him.

Quigley said, "Benson, you and Blake get him over to the bleachers and sort him out."

As they moved away, Cooper shouted back at Tim. "This ain't over. You'll pay for this, Connolly. You're a fuckin' dead man."

After restoring order, Quigley brushed off his slacks and retrieved his clipboard.

"There'll be no workout today. Tomorrow, Brother Frank will take over the track team till the end of the season."

Team members protested. Tim threw his arms in the air.

"No, coach. No. This is wrong. Brother Frank? Jaysus, ye can't be serious, Coach. This gets worse and worse."

As Gina walked up behind Tim, she overheard the conversation. The team continued to grumble, confused and angry. Quigley raised his hand to shush Tim and the others.

"Please. Quiet down. I hope you all give him your full cooperation and show him the dedication and respect you've shown me. Thank you, gentlemen. That will be all." His voice began to crack. "It has been a pleasure working with you. Good luck to you all."

Quigley turned away from the group to compose himself. The other members of the team left the track, most wondering what would happen to the team with Brother Frank in charge.

Tim followed him.

"I won't run for him, Coach. I won't. I trust ye. I know ye'r a good man. He's not."

Quigley pulled him aside. Gina followed to keep within earshot. "Look, Tim, you've got the AAU Championships in two months," he said. "You need to focus on that right now, understand?"

Tim looked at Gina and noticed her concern. She shook her head.

"This is some major-league bullshit, Coach," said Gina. She then spied Cooper, Benson, and Blake by the bleachers. Cooper saw her looking at him and flipped her off.

Quigley focused only on Tim. "Don't worry, Tim," he said. "I'll keep my eye on you. I'll give you the workouts you'll need to be ready."

Tim nodded his head despondently, then turned to Gina. "I've some things to do . . . talk to some people. I'll see ye tomorrow, Gina." He turned to Quigley. "Coach . . . " Tim didn't finish his thought. He just waved his hands in the air and left in a hurry.

Gina turned to Quigley. "You're a good man, Coach. Somebody's screwed you over. It ain't fair."

Quigley responded with a sly grimace. "Fair? Yeah . . . fair." Downcast, he looked around at the empty field and noticed scattered equipment that hadn't been put back in the shed. "Gina, before you leave, would you mind grabbing those two javelins and the starting block and bringing them over to the equipment shed? I'll grab the two hurdles."

Gina gathered the equipment and carried it to the shed, while Quigley walked to the far side of the track to retrieve the hurdles. Cooper, Blake, and Benson saw Gina walking alone. Cooper pointed at her.

"Check this out." He looked back at Quigley moving in the other direction. "Looks like the gimp's leaving. Follow me. Time for some payback on that bitch."

"I want no part of this, Cooper," Blake said. "Count me out."

"Get lost then, chickenshit. And don't even bother coming near us no more."

Blake retreated in a hurry, chased down Quigley, and pointed to the equipment shed. Quigley dropped the hurdles and hurried toward the shed.

Gina had just dropped the javelins and the starting blocks inside when Cooper and Benson appeared in the doorway. Cooper closed the door behind them.

"What are you two assholes up to?" Gina asked. Benson circled behind her, grabbed her arms, and held them while Cooper lunged at her and smacked her face.

"What's the matter, bitch?" said Cooper. "Not so tough now, are you?" He slapped her again across the face with an open hand, then with a backhand. Gina's nose started bleeding, and tears welled in her eyes.

Cooper tore open her jersey and exposed her breasts. "Why, lookee here Benson. She ain't a 'he' after all! Grab a feel."

Benson smiled lasciviously and grabbed at one of her breasts. Gina screamed, kicked, and twisted in terror.

"Get off me, you scumbags!" Just then, Quigley crashed through the door.

"What's going on here?" he said. "Hey! Get your hands off her." Quigley rushed Cooper, who violently tossed him aside. Quigley made a second run at him, but Cooper picked up a javelin and thrust it into Quigley's abdomen who staggered and then fell to his knees, his hands holding the javelin.

"Christ. I'm hurt," he groaned as blood spurted from his wound. Benson released Gina and gaped in shock. Gina rushed to Quigley and held his shoulder.

"Oh, my God! Coach!" she shrieked.

Panicked, Benson shouted, "Cooper! What'd you do?"

Cooper's face was covered with sweat, his mouth white with spittle.

"He asked for it. You saw it. He attacked me. I was just defending myself." Agitated and confused, Benson grabbed Cooper's arm.

"Let's get the hell out of here," he shouted. Cooper staggered backward for a moment. Then he and Benson bolted out the door, just as Blake arrived. Cooper shoved him aside as he and Benson sprinted across the field.

Gina sat for a panicky moment weeping over Quigley's slumped body. Then she pulled the javelin from Quigley's abdomen and placed a piece of her torn shirt on his wound.

"I'm pressing on his wound, Blake. You, run. Move your ass. Get help as fast as you can. I'll stay with Coach."

Blake darted from the shed, passing Cooper and Benson as he rushed to call an ambulance for Quigley.

Chapter Forty-Four

DARK CIRCLES STILL SHADOWED HIS EYES, and old bruises marked his skin, but Terence was regaining lost weight and strength. At first, he was receiving the usual paltry amount of disgusting food served on filthy platters—pasty, maggot-filled potatoes, overcooked, mushy carrots or beans, and rancid meat. McQuarrie, however, started filling Terence's plate with cleaner, better food. Terence was grateful for the decent treatment. It didn't matter to him if McQuarrie helped him out of the goodness of his heart, or simply to keep an IRA bullet from penetrating the back of *his* head. What mattered was that Terence was eating better and feeling better.

Now, in the second week of May, he began a calisthenics regime in his cell—pushups, sit-ups, stretching, and running in place. As he was off his hunger strike, he had access to the exercise yard again, where he would walk vigorously, hoping to increase his leg strength and lung capacity.

When Terence finally informed McCahill that he wanted in on the escape, McCahill replied, "Perfect timing, lad!" He told Terence that the plan was near completion. A prison organizing committee, with help from outside volunteers, had mapped out the escape routes inside the prison walls, from the corridors to the main gate. Once outside, well-armed IRA lads would gather the escapees in cars and lorries and rush them to safe houses in Armagh. In the event anyone separated from the pack, or Plan A failed, escapees would have coded maps directing them along multiple routes from Maze to safety. McCahill mentioned that timing was everything.

"The only delay now is the weapons. Once our fellas smuggle in the necessary pistols," McCahill said, "the game will be on." The escape was planned for a Sunday, he continued, since many of the more experienced guards spent Sundays with their families and those on duty seemed to relax more than usual. The committee had been methodical and thorough, laboring to anticipate every conceivable pitfall. They knew they would have only one chance. If it failed, they would not get another.

Chapter Forty-Five

TIM AND GINA EMERGED from the fifth-floor elevator, walked the hall, and entered Quigley's room. Quigley lay unconscious in a private room, the air thick with disinfectant. Still in critical condition, he was hooked up to an IV and a ventilator, whose rhythmic wheezing punctuated the silence. Quigley's wife, Linda, a slim, gray-haired, well-dressed woman, sat next to the bed, holding his hand. She rose when she saw Tim and Gina.

She took Gina's hand and whispered, "You saved John's life. Thank you so very much."

"He saved mine first." Gina said. "I owe him. He's a good man. I hate to see him like this." Tim looked at Quigley, and his eyes filled with tears. Linda turned and spoke softly to him.

"I am so happy to meet you, Tim. I have heard so much about you. This must be hard for you, along with everything else . . . " She stopped and said, "I'm so sorry."

Tim, lips pressed tightly, nodded his appreciation. Linda sat next to Quigley, picked up his hand, and gave it a soft kiss. "Johnny and I have had a rough time recently," she said. "He told me just a week ago that he had made important, necessary changes in his life to save our marriage . . . and now—now this." She shook her head. "Have they caught the boys who did this?"

"Not yet," said Gina.

In the far corner of the hospital room, a ceiling-mounted television without sound showed Bridget Connolly delivering a portion of her Belfast speech on the NBC Nightly News, but neither Tim nor Gina noticed. When Linda turned back to Quigley and squeezed his hand, she seemed to drift away from the conversation. Tim shrugged, then tilted his head to Gina, indicating that this might be the time to leave. Gina shook her head and tapped Linda's hand.

"I hope you don't mind my asking, ma'am, but what the hell happened between you two? You both seem like really nice people."

Her directness surprised Tim, and Linda too, but she seemed quite willing to respond. Without hesitation, she looked directly at Gina and told her that these things sometimes happen as married people grow older and change from what they were, but for her and Quigley, it was different.

"Johnny had been a good husband and a terrific father to our two children, Laura and Bob. Laura is twenty-eight, a real estate broker with two children of her own. Bob is a thirty-year-old travel agent, single, something of a world traveler. But Johnny? Johnny and I were fine until the kids went to college. With them gone, he didn't have as much to occupy his mind, you know, like being involved with their afternoon and weekend sports and other activities. Gradually, old issues started surfacing. I didn't notice it much at first, but he started to double and triple up on his nightly cocktails; then, he got very drunk at a few neighborhood parties and acted strange. He grossed out some people, insulted others. The kicker, I guess, was the night he was inducted into the Fordham University Track and Field Hall of Fame. Their current track coach showed some of Johnny's old film and made a big fuss about what a phenomenal runner he was back in the day. After that night, he went into a serious tailspin, frequent benders. I tried to reach him, but he wouldn't talk about it. He refused marriage counseling, saying he could sort it out on his own. I finally sought counseling myself.

"My therapist seemed to think he was embittered by a profound sense of loss. She said, 'Look at it from his vantage point: it wasn't just the loss of a healthy leg. It was the loss of his dreams. With a single bullet, the war took away all he ever wanted—a chance to be an Olympic champion. And it had been right there for him, just within his reach. And it slipped away.'

"So, he felt like a failure, much more so than I ever realized. Over time, he got lost in the bottle, as they say. He was fired from a good job he'd had for twenty years because he started missing days, showing up late, or just hungover and making mistakes. He only got a second job because an old friend helped him out. Then he lost that one. The job at St. Jude's fell into his lap because they were desperate, and they pay so damn little that no one else wanted the position.

"Anyway, five months ago, I gave up and filed for divorce. Johnny moved out and found his own place." Linda paused and took a deep breath. She looked at both Gina and Tim, dry-eyed, her voice stronger now. "I love him, and I tried to hang in there, but he was dragging me down. I figured he had to swim or drown. Me too. Sounds harsh, but that's what it came down to. Then, suddenly, he started to 'swim'—and I think you two young people had everything in the world to do with it." Linda leaned over and took Gina by the hand, and then Tim. "Thank you both so much, from the bottom of my heart. I mean it," she said calmly.

Gina shook her head as if to clear out a nest of spiders. "Whew, ma'am! That's some heavy, heavy shh . . . ah, heavy stuff." Her reaction lifted Linda from her seriousness into an expected fit of laughter. Tim let out a deep breath. He was struggling to grapple with one emotion before Gina hurled him into another, then another. It was very confusing.

Linda calmed herself. "Okay, you two get going. I have to keep an eye on this guy here."

"Yes ma'am. We'll be back soon, Mrs. Quigley," said Tim. "Please let us know as soon as he is awake."

"Yes, of course," she said. "Now skedaddle. Thank you both for coming."

Once outside the hospital, Tim looked at Gina, somewhat bewildered.

"That was a stunner. I never expected to hear Mrs. Quigley tell ye the whole tale. Did ye?"

"Of course I did. Why the hell do you think I asked her? I could tell she was dyin' to spill her guts. Geez, Tim! I'm realizing it's not just you Irish who are so damn thick. It's men in general." Changing the subject, Gina asked, "What are you doing tomorrow?"

"Coach said he wants me to train all out for the AAU," said Tim. "So that's what I'll do. But training with Brother Frank?" Tim shook his head. "Hell no."

Then he asked her, "How're ye now after what happened at the field?"

Gina said, "Still upset. No. More angry than upset. I've never been attacked like that in my life. I'll tell you, Tim, if I had a gun, I would've killed them two bastards. But they'll get what's coming to them. I'm sure of that. I just hope I'm there to see it.

Chapter Forty-Six

THE FOLLOWING MONDAY, TIM was on the track alone, stopwatch in hand, completing his day's training. While other team members were straggling onto the field for their warm-ups, Tim strode powerfully down the far straightaway, cruising around the turn, finishing smooth, fast, and strong.

Brother Frank and the rest of the team arrived at the field as Tim crossed the finish line. Breathing heavily, he took one slow lap around the track, then jogged over to his equipment bag, took off his spikes, and pulled on his sweats.

Brother Frank approached Tim, positioning himself between him and the rest of the team.

"Where do you think you're going, Connolly?" he asked.

"I'm finished, Brother," said Tim. "I never do more than three reps of eight-hundreds at that pace."

Brother Frank laughed sardonically and turned to the rest of the team. "Will somebody tell Mr. Connolly here that there is a new coach in town, and that things are going to be done differently from now on?"

Tim said, "What's the point, Brother? I've done well enough with Mr. Quigley's workouts."

"The point, Connolly, is who's in charge here."

Tim shrugged and shook his head as he laced his training shoes.

"You challenging me, young man?" Again, Brother Frank

turned to address the rest of the team. "I repeat. Things are going to be different now! There will be no more of the special treatment shown to a certain few. We will be doing things my way, and everyone will be treated the same." He turned to Tim. "Now Connolly, put your spikes back on and do two more eight-hundreds."

Tim ignored him, rising slowly after lacing his shoes. His teammates looked stunned. Spikes in hand, he took two steps and stood directly in front of Brother Frank. Tim stared calmly into his eyes. Oddly, at this moment, he remembered one of Great-Grandfather Brian's favorite tales about the power of the evil eye, the one about Celtic chieftain, Balor of the Evil Eye, who only uncovered his deadly right eye in battle, unleashing a power no enemy warrior could survive.

Staring into the eyes of Brother Frank, Tim felt Balor's mortal power coursing through his veins and into his own eyes. When he violently clapped his spikes together, Brother Frank, who had been clenching and unclenching his fists, flinched and took a step back. Blake and the rest of the track team watched, transfixed. As Brother Frank snarled and raised his right hand to strike a blow, Tim stood firm, his eyes burning pure hatred into his enemy's eyes. Brother Frank froze, then slowly lowered his hand, baffled and discomfited.

Tim turned sharply and walked away. Team members, stunned by what they had witnessed, whispered in disbelief.

"Get back here, Connolly," said Brother Frank, trying to rally. "I'm warning you." Tim strode briskly off the track toward the locker room. Behind him, he heard Brother Frank's cracking voice. "That's it, hot shot! You're off the team. You're through!"

Tim waved his right hand without turning around.

Blake watched Tim's challenge and departure intently. He glanced at Brother Frank, then gathered his gear and rushed off the field, following Tim.

"Tyrone!" Brother Frank shouted. "Where the hell do you think you're going? Get back here."

Blake ignored him.

His tone suddenly changed. "Don't do this, Tyrone! Please don't do this!" Confused and upset, he barked at the other members of the team. "Okay, everybody on the track. Twenty-minute run, and that's it."

Blake, meanwhile, caught up to Tim.

"Connolly. You done the right thing, man." Tim kept walking, trying to ignore him. "Wait, a second, Tim, will you?" Blake pleaded.

Tim stopped and faced him.

"First, I—I want you to know . . . how sorry I am. For everything," said Blake.

Tim lowered his head. He sensed Blake's pain for the first time.

"No, need, lad. I could tell ye weren't really like them."

"As for him . . . " Blake said, pointing to Brother Frank.

Tim started walking away again. "Don't want to hear it." Blake moved in front of Tim to confront him.

"Please, Tim. You got to. You're the only one who knows."

Tim looked at his spikes and clapped them, brooding.

"I'd never say anything."

Blake said, "Thanks, man. I mean it." Then he lost his composure. "I didn't . . . I mean I never—uh, I don't know what to do, Tim. Never did. He scares the shit out of me. It's like the bastard owns me. I hate him. What he's done to me. The beatings, grabbing me, forcing me, all the time. I'd like to fuckin' kill him."

"I don't blame you," said Tim, growing angrier. "Me too." He stared at Blake for a few simmering seconds, then said, "Maybe we can do something to stop him. I've got an idea. Let's talk about this . . ."

As Tim and Blake faded in the distance together, Brother Frank tracked them, wondering what the last fifteen minutes of his life had just cost him.

Chapter Forty-Seven

THAT EVENING, AS TIM DEVOURED his lasagna, Mary watched him anxiously, expecting some news. Tim had been strangely silent all evening, the day's events crackling like live wires inside his head. Mary finally brushed Gary's elbow to force his attention. She nodded toward Tim, and they both looked at him until he noticed them. Catching them plotting, he smiled.

"Ah! I know what ye'r thinking. Wonderin' what's going on, eh?" Tim paused to finish chewing the lasagna in his mouth. "Well, Blake and I are working on something. It's personal with him, and he doesn't want me talking about it. Anyway, we won't know anything until tomorrow."

Just then, the phone in the living room rang. Gary left the table and answered it.

"Yes. He's here," Gary said. "Tim, it's for you!"

Tim took the phone. "Who is it?" he whispered to his uncle..

Gary shrugged his shoulders. "Some woman."

"Hello. Tim Connolly here."

"Tim, this is Linda Quigley. John has regained consciousness. He wants to see you."

Tim smiled and raised his voice. "Oh, that's grand news, ma'am. I'll be right there." He hung up the phone. "I've got to get to the hospital. Coach is awake."

Gary rose from his chair, "I'll take you, Marty." Tim and Mary, startled, looked at him. Gary awkwardly corrected himself, "I meant *Tim.* Tim. Let me get my jacket." Mary smiled at her husband and gently touched his cheek as he passed her.

###

When Tim entered the hospital room thirty minutes later, Linda was sitting next to Quigley. He had been in the hospital for ten days. The first week had been precarious. Two separate operations were required to patch his damaged organs, while the pain-killing drugs had wrapped him in a mental cocoon. But he was beginning to show signs of recovery. Though still hooked up to an IV, he was off the ventilator. Tim sat next to Quigley on the side of the bed opposite Linda.

"It's good to see ye awake, Coach. We were all worried," Tim said.

Quigley replied in a strained, raspy voice. "How's Gina?"

"She's fine, Coach," said Tim. "Pretty angry though at what happened. However, she's truly grateful to ye for saving her." Quigley waved his hand and smiled.

"Cooper and Benson? Those two dipshits?" asked Quigley. Turning to Linda, he said, "Pardon my French."

"No sign of them," Tim said.

Quigley shook his head. "Listen . . . Most important . . . You . . . " He struggled to speak beyond a whisper. "Keep training. You can win this thing."

Tim said, "Coach, I've been kicked off the team."

"What?" said Quigley.

"And Blake quit," said Tim. The Coach coughed and tried to catch his breath.

"What the hell?" he said. "What for?" Quigley started to get restless. Linda moved over to calm him. She lifted his head and slightly adjusted his pillow, then held the back of his head while he took a sip of water.

Tim explained, "Coach, this Brother Frank is a . . . a pervert. Blake . . . "

"He's a nasty bastard, that's for sure." Quigley turned to Linda again. "Sorry . . . my French." Turning back to Tim. "But it's you I'm concerned about right now, Tim." Quigley closed his eyes and took a deep breath.

Tim tried to continue. "Yes, sir. But about Brother Frank. I . . . uh—you should know, Blake and I . . . "

"Stop, Tim. Listen," said Quigley. "The AAU Championship is an *open* meet. You don't have to be on a school team. We'll get you entered . . . " He looked over at Linda.

She said, "Absolutely. Just tell me who to call."

Quigley took her hand and looked to Tim. "Tim, this is my wife, Linda."

Tim said, "I know, Coach. We've met."

"The most wonderful woman . . . God ever created." Quigley broke into tears. "What I have put her through . . ."

Controlling her emotions, Linda said, "Stop it, John. Not now." She looked at Tim and joked, "He always gets sentimental when someone sticks a javelin in him." Tim smiled as Quigley clenched and kissed Linda's hand.

"I better go. Good to see ye getting better, Coach. I'll check in tomorrow," Tim said.

"Okay. You do your schoolwork and stay clear of Brother Frank," said Quigley. "You've got about six weeks before the trials. Follow the workouts I'll send you."

"Will do, Coach."

Chapter Forty-Eight

TIM MET GINA IN THE MAIN HALLWAY near the principal's office. She pulled a peanut-butter-and-jelly sandwich out of her backpack and started chewing. She offered Tim a bite. He declined. Tim looked at his watch several times. Just then, two police officers strode through the main entrance.

"They're here," said Tim.

"Cops? Is this why you got me here? Son of a bitch! What's up?" she asked.

"Just wait," said Tim.

As the police marched down the hall, dozens of curious students followed them, then gathered outside the athletic director's office. Tim and Gina joined the crowd and peered in the office. The officers were standing in front of Brother Frank. He was waving his arms and arguing with the police, his rosary beads flailing in his right.

"This is an outrage," he shouted. "I'm a Christian Brother and the athletic director here. What the hell do you think you're doing?"

The shorter police officer stood in front of Brother Frank, raised his hand, and tried to calm him. Meanwhile, the taller officer walked behind, cuffed him, and read him his rights. Brother Frank's face pulsed and reddened in anger, "This is an outrage," he repeated. "This is a terrible mistake." The assembled crowd became louder and more animated.

"Take him away! Lock him up!" one student hidden safely in the crowd gleefully shouted. Cheers and laughter. Then Father Kenney arrived. He was silent and solemn as Brother Frank struggled and protested. Standing with Father Kenney were Blake and his parents. Blake had a byzantine grin on his face, a portrait of bitter satisfaction.

Seeing Kenney nearby, Brother Frank shouted.

"Jim, do something. Stop this!" The priest stared ahead, expressionless and mute. As the police escorted him down the hall, Brother Frank turned to Blake and pleaded, "Tyrone, I'm sorry. I truly never meant . . ."

At that moment, Blake's weeping mother broke away from her son and husband and confronted Brother Frank and screamed, "What kind of man are you? You're supposed to be a man of God. We trusted you! You're a disgrace. You're nothing but a filthy pig!" She smacked him across the face, then tried to hit him again, but Blake's silent, stone-faced father pulled her back as the police moved Frank away from her.

"So sorry . . . " he wailed tearfully.

"Filthy animal! You bastard!" she shouted as the trio disappeared down the hall. When they were gone, Gina grinned at Tim.

"Well, son of a bitch!" she said. "You did this, didn't ya?"

"Aye," Tim whispered, angry and unsmiling. "But ye helped. Ye showed me, lass, how to stand up to people like him." He spotted Blake looking in his direction. They nodded approvingly at each other.

###

Six months later, a jury found Brother Frank guilty of multiple counts of sexual assault of a minor. Blake's testimony was supported by two other current students and twelve former students who shared their bitter tales of abuse. The jury found him guilty and likely to be sentenced to twenty-five years in jail for his offenses.

Unexpectedly, the presiding judge, a rabid Opus Dei Catholic, vacated the verdict when diocesan lawyers presented evidence that one of the jurors had herself been a rape victim and her judgment, therefore, could not be trusted. The judge further refused a retrial on the spurious grounds that any future jury pool would be tainted by knowledge of the circumstances of the previous trial. Brother Frank's attorneys then requested a directed judgment to have his record be expunged. Judgment was granted.

Wary of returning him to St. Jude's, the bishop of the Queens diocese contacted some old seminary friends and eventually secured a position for Brother Frank in a prestigious Christian Brothers Academy in Ames, Iowa. Brother Frank settled anonymously into his new position for the first two years. In his third year, however, student and parent complaints started reaching the diocese's lawyers. Before complaints reached the courts, however, the Superior-General of the Christian Brothers preemptively assigned Brother Frank to a remote missionary school outside Nairobi, Kenya. While no reports of unacceptable behavior reached the authorities in Kenya, Brother Frank mysteriously disappeared within months of his arrival. He was never seen or heard from again.

Chapter Forty-Nine

AFTER BROTHER FRANK WAS ARRESTED, Tim and Gina celebrated at "Izzy's Diner" over hamburgers and milkshakes.

"The look on his bloody face was priceless," Tim said. "And sure, wasn't this the tough guy, this whinging, sadistic bully, waving his rosary beads in the air, sobbing like a baby."

"I always figured him for a damned pervert," Gina said. "And what he done to you!" She placed her hand softly on Tim's face. Tim touched her hand. They stopped talking and looked at one another as though for the first time.

Tim broke the gaze and smiled. Gina looked down and away. "Gina, I . . . uh . . ."

"Don't say anything, Greenhorn," Gina said. "You'll only embarrass yourself. And me!" At that, Tim slid out of his side of the booth and sat next to her. He put his arms around her. Gina responded with enthusiasm. They kissed passionately and became increasingly frisky, forcing Izzy to come over to their table.

"That's enough, you two," he said. "Either calm down or take it elsewhere."

Tim and Gina laughed, paid the bill, and left the shop. When they arrived at Gina's house, they scurried to her finished basement since her father was asleep upstairs. They stumbled as they hastily removed and tossed their clothes, before landing awkwardly on the couch. Gina quickly reached operational nudity and attitude. Tim's trousers and shorts, though, knotted his ankles and locked his legs together, causing him to flail alligator-like between Gina's hoisted legs, which were waving wildly in the air. In less than a minute, Tim felt tremors rumbling through his body, from his feet to his brain. He suddenly felt like the top of his head had been sawed off. Gina, meanwhile, giggled like a maniac, waving her arms like she'd just won the lottery.

Tim sputtered afterward, "Gina, Jeez, I'm sorry. I've never done this before. I, uh . . ."

"That's obvious, Greenhorn. Just shows you're fast at everything, not just running." She laughed even more. "By the way, in case you're wondering, Speedy Gonzales, I'm still . . . how shall I say . . . 'unblemished.' You never made it to the finish line."

Tim laughed, embarrassed. "Again, Gina . . . so sorry.

"That's okay, Tim. Just shows we're gonna need more practice in this area, so I can help you with your pacing, so I can scratch this damn virgin thing off my to-do list." Tim smiled and gently pulled her to him.

"That's fine with me, lass. I think ye'll be an excellent coach."

Chapter Fifty

TIM RECEIVED HIS FATHER'S LETTER at the end of May, unaware that Terence had since abandoned his hunger strike and was now part of the H-Block escape team. The letter deepened Tim's sadness, but his father's spirit in the face of terror and death inspired Tim. Yes, he would partner in spirit with his Da. He would also use his upcoming races to honor his father and, where possible, denounce the abuses at H-Block. This emotion immediately fueled the intensity of his workouts. He knew that he needed to be faster and stronger to win.

Throughout the month of May, Tim, Gina, and Blake trained together. Blake enjoyed hanging out with Tim and Gina. Now that he was released from the thrall of Brother Frank and Cooper, Blake's sullen attitude lightened. He refused to talk about Brother Frank, though. He was content to let the lawyers carry the weight, and Gina and Tim never questioned him.

Gina did ask him directly one day about his time with Cooper and Benson.

"Why would an intelligent guy like you could hang out with two assholes like that?"

Blake shook his head. "I don't know. Not sure. They were big shots. Being with them made me feel, what, more important? Accepted? Maybe tough, or protected? I don't know."

Gina never raised the topic again.

Neither Gina nor Tim comprehended the depth of Blake's confusion and pain. Soon after Brother Frank's earliest "attentions," Blake had started experiencing sleep and eating disorders, anxiety, and even self-injury. In one case of cutting, he tried to disguise the cuts as a tattoo carved into his forearm. Until recently, he had been blaming himself. Brother Frank had successfully exploited Blake's shame, swearing him to secrecy, threatening or beating him to keep him from ever speaking out.

"Who would believe a black boy before a clergyman—a respected Christian Brother?"

Often after sex, Brother Frank would force Blake to pray with him to cleanse themselves of "their sin." While Blake felt vindicated by his and Tim's successful plot to expose and imprison the monster, he had yet to plumb the unexplored chasms of shame and vexed sexuality. Was he straight or gay? He dated girls and enjoyed heavy petting, but the specter haunted him. Worse, he felt like a homeless creature trapped in a storm with no place to go, no one to protect him. Not even his father. Though his mother tended to him like her wounded child, his father, once doting and proud of his boy, was suddenly distant, aloof. A bad man had stolen his son's childhood, causing wounds that might never fully heal, and he had gone mute and deaf to his son's trauma. Blake would take the first shaky steps toward recovery by himself.

But for now? Now, he would run, and run, and find solace in the company of two wounded friends who'd adopted him at this fraught moment in his life.

###

The high school track meets for the remainder of the school year were closed to the three of them because St. Jude's had disbanded the team. They now had no coach, and no one wanted the job. St Jude's administrators and alumni were also reeling from the scandal, embarrassed by the negative publicity, and unnerved by pending lawsuits that accused them of harboring a sadistic pedophile.

Gina, Tim, and Blake, meanwhile, were enjoying their free-wheeling, independent workouts. Quigley convinced Gina to compete in the AAU trials, just to see how she stacked up against the country's best. Blake continued working out with Tim. He also planned to compete, especially now that he was being recruited by college coaches from Morgan State University, Temple University, and the University of Southern California, which had become his clear first choice.

Graduation day took place the last Sunday of May. Tim, Gina, and Blake did not attend. Tim's courses transferred to Mercy College in Sligo, from which he received his "Established Learning Certificate." Tim had never liked St. Jude's. His only attachment to the place consisted of Gina, Quigley, and now Blake. Gina had never liked the school or anyone in it either . . . until she met Tim. She wouldn't have attended graduation under any circumstances. As for Blake? Not a chance. For all three, it was an open-and-shut case of "good riddance."

The trio's sole focus for the upcoming weeks would be preparing for the AAU trials, and then the championship race, *if* they made it through the trials. The district trials would take place at Van Cortlandt Park, a popular Bronx location for city runners that featured a "fast" rubber composition track. The regional trials were planned for the Wilbur Cross Athletic Complex. Its running track, next to the scenic Mill River, was situated in a posh suburb of New Haven, Connecticut. The national championships would be held at Randall's Island Stadium in New York City, where Tim had set his state record.

Chapter Fifty-One

FOR TWO MONTHS AFTER THEIR APPEARANCE at the Belfast rally, Bridget and Maeve received calls from newspapers and local radio stations. Their anti-H-Block crusade had successfully enlisted thousands of Catholic and Protestant women from the north and south to their cause. Their "road show" had by now earned them a measure of celebrity. In their encounters with the media, Bridget persuaded with her charm, intelligence, and her passion. Maeve, meanwhile, persuaded with her mastery of the data, but also with her brash manner. She stirred the occasional on-air uproar with her frequently censored comments, but her demeanor only enhanced the duo's popularity. At one call-in radio show, a Galway man suggested that the two women would better serve the world by tending to their domestic chores rather than yapping all around Ireland on subjects they knew nothing about. Maeve's response, touting the staggering ignorance of the caller, was littered with a string of obscenities, only half of which were successfully censored by the engineer before they filled the airwaves.

After that show in the middle of June, Bridget received a phone call from an official with *Dail Eireann*, inviting her and Maeve to Dublin to meet with the Minister for Foreign Affairs the following Monday. After checking with Maeve, Bridget accepted the invitation, hoping this might provide an important boost to their campaign.

The train from Sligo to Dublin gave them three hours to gather their notes and refine their presentation. When they arrived at Connolly Station at 10 a.m., they were met by a tall, thin, black-suited chauffeur who drove them to St. Stephen's Green and escorted them into the luxurious Shelbourne Hotel. The chauffeur assured them that their room, meals, and transportation were covered by the government.

"Good feckin thing," Maeve said. "I'd have to sell me children into slavery to pay for all this."

He said he would return in two hours to deliver them to their meeting at the Castle.

Maeve marveled at the suite's amenities. She was especially taken with the luxurious bathroom. "Will ye look at this now, Bridget? A giant, deep tub, a walk-in shower with a glass door . . . And sure enough, can ye believe it? A bloody bidet! I'll be damned if I don't give that little fella a test drive before we leave."

Bridget stretched out on the plush king-size bed, impressed by the elegant wall hangings and heavy, linen-pleated draperies. She reflected on the bitter irony of the situation. Here she was, being feted by bigwigs in Dublin and lounging in luxury, all while her husband was starving, wrapped in a dirty blanket, isolated in a harsh, cold cell. Exhausted and upset, she closed her eyes and took a short but deep nap.

The one-hour meeting with the Minister of Foreign Affairs went much as Bridget and Maeve had expected—the usual blowsy compliments for their commitment to a worthy cause, the blah, blah pride of their nation for their courage, his "absolute promise" to raise the issue with his British counterpart, and his assurance that the Taoiseach would be "very strong" on this matter when he spoke with Prime Minister Thatcher.

Bridget was profoundly unimpressed with the minister's unctuous, patronizing manner. Maeve shifted restlessly in her chair throughout the conversation, straining not to express exactly what she was thinking. They offered a perfunctory "thank you" to the minister when he stood to show them the door.

Once in the hall, Maeve exploded. "I've never, in me entire life, heard such a wagonload of patronizing and platitudinous horseshit." She shook her head. "Let's get back to the hotel and crack that feckin minibar."

Chapter Fifty-Two

IN THE FINAL WEEKS BEFORE THE AAU Championships, Tim did long morning runs through Forest Park's wooded trails, which were cushioned with rotted leaves and wood chips. Squawking crows and foraging squirrels ignored him as he moved in quiet harmony with the soft rhythms of this place.

His afternoon sprint workouts on the track, on the other hand, were all business.

The day's regimen ended with bench presses, squats, toe raises, and curls in the weight room. Concerned about the increasing rigor of his daily workout schedule, Quigley invited Tim to his home two weeks after he was released from the hospital.

"You're peaking. Be careful," said Quigley. "Here is where you need more rest. You have to begin to taper. If you don't cut back at this point, Tim, you risk injury. So be sure you rest and relax—take off every fourth day and reduce your number of high-intensity repetitions."

Quigley also instructed him on race strategy, letting him know especially that he was now running against men, not high school boys, and that sometimes they played dirty. "They can use their bigger bodies to push you outside, block your maneuvering, step on your heels, or box you in. So, pay attention. Be aware of their moves from the start, especially on the turns." Finally, he warned Tim not to get awestruck by the hoopla, the big crowds. "Think of this as just another race, and be ready," Quigley said. "You are ready, aren't you?"

"Yes, sir, I am." Tim said. "I am."

###

Van Cortland Park was New York City's third largest park—eleven hundred acres in the Bronx and dedicated to all kinds of outdoor recreation, from cross country running to golf, hiking, swimming, lacrosse, rugby, soccer, swimming, tennis, and track and field.

On Saturday, June 25, the park's center of attention was the AAU district trials, which would determine which athletes would proceed to the regional trials the following Saturday—Independence Day weekend in New Haven.

The competition from this point would be more difficult than anything Tim, Gina, and Blake had ever experienced. Only a few of the premier runners from Eastern regional high schools would be competing, and they were not expected to go very far. The favored competitors were mostly elite runners and field event performers from the nation's universities and prestigious athletic clubs, like the NYAC or Boston Athletic Clubs. Blake opted to compete in the four-hundred-meter trials, while Tim would compete, as expected, in the eight-hundred. There were two morning heats in each race. Each heat had eight runners, and the top three from each heat would compete in the final heat, in the late afternoon.

Blake ran a splendid race—his personal best—against tough competition, qualifying for the afternoon heat by a millisecond, grabbing third place by a well-timed lean at the finish line. By the finals that afternoon, Blake was physically and emotionally spent. He finished a respectable fifth overall, but he was out of the hunt.

Tim's morning heat was notable only for the ease with which he finished in first place, advancing to the afternoon final. The main obstacle to his afternoon victory was the pileup that occurred after the 110-meter mark as runners left their starting lanes and jostled one another, fighting for the inside lane. Tim, who held back at the start, saw the mess unfolding on the first turn as runners' legs became entangled, elbows flew, and bodies tumbled on the track. He deftly moved to an outside lane to avoid the crashing bodies, though he was forced to hurdle two runners who fell into his path. From that point, his path to victory was assured, and Tim broke the tape, comfortably securing his spot for the next week's regionals.

Gina finished third in the shot put but didn't qualify for the javelin. She stepped over the line and fouled out of the competition with her best throw. Gina was impressed by the quality of the women's competition, especially the two hirsute female German shot-putters—University of Rhode Island exchange students, who placed first and second. She laughingly called them "Hans and Fritz" and said the two women reminded her of Arnold Schwarzenegger in *Conan the Barbarian*. She was not optimistic about her chances in the regionals.

Chapter Fifty-Three

THE ESCAPE PLAN PROCEEDED SLOWLY and methodically. Still no date.

Though he was anxious for the day to arrive, Terence used the time to train, to continue to rebuild himself. He had been a fine athlete in his youth. His quickness and endurance on the pitch, whether football or hurling, were legendary in north Sligo, as was his willingness to engage in what his coaches called "extracurricular protection of his team and himself." Terence was now doing as many as a hundred pushups and an equal number of sit-ups in his cell throughout each day. He was also running in place for several twenty-minute intervals each day. In the exercise yard, he and McCahill used their entire break to jog and do calisthenics. The delays also gave Terence the necessary time to learn his specific responsibilities during the escape.

Finally, the big event came. On Sunday, July 2, Terence, McCahill, and thirty-five other prisoners followed their leader, Gerry Murphy, and quickly seized control of H7. They took eleven "screws" hostage at gunpoint and prevented them from triggering an alarm. Several guards resisted. McCahill brought down one resisting officer by slamming an office chair over his head. Terence took that guard's baton and leveled a second attacking guard with a vicious blow to the temple. Furious, he continued to hit the guard savagely after he fell. Two prisoners dragged a wild-eyed Terence away from the unconscious guard and labored to calm him. The prisoners quickly and successfully took control of H7 without an alarm being raised. Prisoners, Terence among them, stripped uniforms from a dozen guards, bound their hands and feet with duct tape, and donned their uniforms.

Shortly after the hostages were secured, the lorry delivering laundry supplies arrived at the entrance to H7. The escapees, now in guards' uniforms, surrounded the lorry and took the driver and his partner hostage at gunpoint. Murphy calmly told the driver that his lorry was being requisitioned for the escape. He told him what route to take and how to react if challenged by guards or the RUC. While Murphy lay on the floor of the cab with a gun pointed at the driver, Terence and thirty-four prisoners climbed into the back of the lorry. Murphy told the already fear-stricken driver that the cab had been booby trapped with a hand grenade. Just in case.

When the lorry arrived at the main gate of the prison, Terence and eleven other disguised prisoners, jumped out, entered the gatehouse, and took the guards hostage. When a voice responded to the alarm via intercom, Murphy held his gun to the head of a senior guard and told him to say that the alarm had been triggered accidentally. He did. Murphy then had him disarm the emergency sirens and lights.

But then, an unforeseen problem occurred. Guards arriving for the next shift were being corralled one-by-one as hostages. Before long, however, the hostages outnumbered the escapees. Once they assessed their numerical advantage, the guards attacked the prisoners. Punches, kicks, batons, and chairs were flying. Then knives and gunshots. Several escapees and two guards were wounded. One guard was killed. The lorry hurriedly swerved in the direction of the brawl. All but a wounded few prisoners jumped into the back of the moving vehicle.

When they were safely aboard, the lorry driver floored the accelerator, speeding for the main gate. Too late. Two incoming guards had seen the chaos and blocked the gate with their cars. Panic ensued. Terence and other desperate escapees abandoned the lorry, bolted for the fence, scaled it, and ran for their freedom.

Once outside the prison, the escapees faced another unpleasant surprise. None of the expected IRA vehicles or armed support awaited them. Confusion reigned. While some few escapees successfully hijacked guards' cars, most started running, scattering in all directions like ants from a shattered colony. One stolen Toyota screeched to a halt near Terence and McCahill as they sprinted down the hill. The driver, Bobby O'Neill, told them to jump in back.

Chapter Fifty-Four

THE CONCIERGE HANDED MAEVE a note when she and Bridget returned to the hotel. Frank Furey, host of RTE's *Ireland Today,* had invited them to make a guest appearance that very day on his popular afternoon program.

They accepted immediately, and the chauffeur promptly drove them to the station, where they were prepped with make-up and fitted with microphones. This invitation afforded them with an opportunity to reach their largest audience—all of Ireland, the UK, and possibly even a public radio or television station in the United States.

Bridget was well-versed now in the granular details of the anti-H-Block movement and knew how to eloquently propagate the "absolute necessity for Ireland's women to be involved." This theme was also Maeve's signal to assail male politicians for their callous ineptitude and cowardice, her signature crowd-pleasing riff.

Frank Furey introduced Bridget and Maeve to polite applause from the studio audience as they took their seats around a circular table. Two large TV cameras on dollies circled the desk as Furey questioned them about their movement's aims and actions to date, and their successes. Five minutes into the interview, however, Furey surprised Bridget when he asked her to talk about her husband and her son. Bridget was, by now, accustomed to discussing human rights issues in straightforward social and political terms, detailing the sufferings of the men of H-Block, their families, and their communities, but she never publicly discussed the details of her own family life—her love for Terence and Tim, and her emptiness at being separated from them. She was stunned by the question and seemed disinclined to respond.

"If it's all the same to you, Mr. Furey, there are some things . . ." said Bridget.

"Go ahead, love," whispered Maeve. "This is important."

Bridget looked into her friend's eyes and whispered back, "Maeve, really. I'm not sure about this."

"We're here. Give it a shot. What the hell have ye got to lose?" Maeve delivered her last words to the live audience, which applauded its encouragement.

"Oh my God," said Bridget. "Where to start?"

She began by telling the audience how she met Terence in the eighth grade. They were both thirteen at the time. She admired his cheerful good looks, his athletic build, and his dark, wavy hair. He wasn't very talkative, but he wasn't shy either. Bridget felt he developed his confidence on the pitch. He excelled at Gaelic football and hurling. He was also, unexpectedly—which she loved—an exceptionally fine step dancer. They were friendly in school and went to the same church, and they shared many of the same friends.

Furey probed even further. "When did you fall in love with him?" he asked.

Bridget shook her head, hesitated, and smiled.

"Oh . . . I, uh—I suppose it was the day Terence was injured in a football match," she said. "We were both eighteen. I don't know why, but I waited for him after the game. He was the last one to leave the pitch, and when I saw him limping in my direction, I must have looked at him a certain way, for he just stopped and smiled. He smiled this beautiful, outrageous smile and said, 'Ah, Bridget me love.' Then he limped over to me, and he hugged me and kissed me. We have loved one another since that day. Since that moment, actually."

Bridget paused, then smiled at the memory through her wet eyes. "Me son, Tim, was born two years after we were married. It was a difficult birth, and afterward, I was informed that bearing more children would be dangerous for me. So, we have the one boy. I suppose that made me more protective of him, He is a fine lad—smart, funny, and kind, but otherwise he's a shy young fella. Most of his time is—or *was*, I should say—taken up with school and farm chores, so he does not—or did not, sorry—have a busy social life. He lives now with me sister in New York City . . . temporarily, ye know, during Terence's imprisonment. I have recently heard from his school coach that he has developed an extraordinary gift for running and has become something of a track star. I miss him terribly and am desperate to see him and his Da as soon as I possibly can."

Bridget broke down. Maeve grabbed her hand and squeezed it tightly.

"Thank you for sharing that with us, Mrs. Connolly," said Furey. "Your husband and son are very lucky to have you working for them. I sincerely hope you see them both very soon, and I wish you and Mrs. Grogan the best of luck with your current mission."

Furey turned to the camera. "I would urge all our viewers to join Bridget Connolly's and Maeve Grogan's crusade, so please urge your local representatives to support a halt to the human rights abuses in H-Block and to negotiate an end to the senseless bloodshed in the north. Again, thanks Mrs. Connolly and Mrs. Grogan. That's it for *Ireland Today*, folks. Thank you so much for watching."

Furey shook hands with Bridget and Maeve, repeating his hopes for their success, then left the set to speak with his assistants.

Maeve released Bridget's hand. "Marvelous, me dear. I think we made some strides tonight. I'm starving. You? Let's get something to eat."

"Not really, Maeve. Let's grab something on the train. I'm exhausted. I just want to get home and sleep in me own bed."

Maeve nodded. "I understand completely, of course."

Chapter Fifty-Five

TERENCE AND MCCAHILL SAT NERVOUSLY in the backseat of the hijacked Toyota Corolla. Bobby O'Neill, who had been one of the planners, drove the car at top speed down Eglantine Road.

"Sorry for the cock-up, lads," he said. "We thought we could get out before the shift change, then . . . goddammit, we also thought we had support waiting out here, but . . . shit. We're free for now. Let's stay free. Five more kilometers down the road at a town called Bleary, we're ditching the car in the woods, then it's every man for himself. There will be roadblocks, search parties, and helicopters looking for us in minutes, so when we get there, spread out and take off in different directions."

McCahill turned to Terence and said, "Well, a pleasure knowin' ye, Connolly. Best of luck, and God bless ye." He added, "By the way, did I ever tell ye I was once a priest?"

Terence laughed. "What? Now ye tell me? Really, Pat, who the hell cares? I'd ask ye for a blessing, but certainly it wouldn't be worth much now, eh? Good luck to ye, though, and thanks for all yer help."

When the car stopped, the escaped prisoners scattered. McCahill started running across a wheat field. Terence, still in uniform and a pistol in his jacket, opted to run down the paved road as far and fast as he could, planning to take cover when he spied danger. The Army and the RUC would have activated a cordon of checkpoints for miles around the prison. He could already hear the whirring blades of helicopters in the distance. Terence had studied the map the planners had circulated in preparation for the escape and started running in the direction of Armagh, some forty kilometers south, where the IRA's South Armagh Brigade was operating several safe houses. Terence ran at a strong, steady pace, dashing for cover several times as military vehicles cruised by with searchlights.

After running and walking for more than three hours, Terence felt the adrenaline seeping from his body, replaced by leg- and brain-wearying fatigue. In this state, he became dangerously inattentive to danger signals. Terence decided to leave the main road. He crossed a field and wandered into a forested area, thick with purple heather and sprawling fern. He found a wide-canopied hickory tree, scraped together a bed of fern and fallen leaves in a shallow dugout, and covered himself with a thin blanket of fallen leaves and leafy branches—more for camouflage than warmth. The bone-chilling dampness was no match for Terence's fatigue, and he slept till sunlight.

When he rose, he was covered in dew. He rubbed his hands over his arms and chest, eager to chase the chill and circulate his blood. All that day, Terence wandered in the shadows during intermittent rain. He followed shrouded hiking trails, scuffling through untrodden brush, crushing paths through patches of golden cowslips. As best he could, he tried to stay roughly parallel with the main road. Police and army vehicles routinely traveled north and south in his vicinity. When their sirens blared and their vehicles raced past at high speed, Terence dove for cover, and when they passed him, he suspected bad news for some other escapee.

Chapter Fifty-Six

THOUGH BLAKE WAS NOW OUT of the competition, he was working with Tim—pacing him during his intervals and challenging him during his time trials. Gina worked the stopwatch for them when she wasn't doing her own drills. All three were enjoying the freedom from classes, the fresh air and exercise. Gina, however, was less focused on the outcome of *her* competition. She'd decided several days ago that she would not be attending college, so the championship had become less consequential for her, despite the "full boats" that had been floated her way by several college coaches. She decided not to tell Tim yet about her decision because she was worried about how it might affect him. Or distract him.

But she knew he would understand, especially because of what had happened the previous Monday.

That day, after practice, Gina and Tim had gone for pizza at Vito's Ristorante. They ordered a large pepperoni pizza and two large Cokes. Gina decided to take the four uneaten slices home for her father, who loved Vito's food. She thought it would be a casual opportunity for her father to meet Tim.

When they arrived at the front door, however, they smelled smoke. Once inside, Gina saw smoke billowing from the kitchen, where flames snatched the window curtains and rose from a saucepan. The evaporated contents had scalded the pan, causing acrid smoke to fill the kitchen and living room. While Gina ran quickly through the house, looking for her father, Tim tore down the curtains with a wettened dish towel and dropped them in the sink. He did the same with the saucepan and opened the window to clear the smoke. Gina, meanwhile, found her father in his bedroom, sitting on the edge of his bed, conversing with Maria, his late wife. Seeing Gina, his face opened into a broad smile.

"Hi honey," he said. Gina sat next to him and embraced him, trembling.

"Didn't you smell the smoke, Pop?" she asked him.

"Of course, sweetie," he replied. "I'm making some mushroom soup for your mom. She loves that stuff."

"Oh, Papa," Gina cried as she sat next to her father and rocked him in her strong arms. Tim arrived at the doorway and watched Gina, near tears himself, as she cradled the damaged old man until she could settle him under his covers. Later, when her father was asleep, Gina told Tim she would have to find someone to help care for him. Tim agreed, but without realizing how her decision would affect them.

Chapter Fifty-Seven

JULY 2 WAS A STEAMY SUMMER DAY for the New Haven regionals. Quigley met with Tim before the morning race, telling him not to take the lead but to hang back in second or third place, being certain to save enough for a strong finishing kick to end up in the top three.

"You don't want to show all your cards in this race. You'll need some reserve for the afternoon. This heat can drain your strength. Also, next week's coaches and runners will be watching you. We don't want to show them everything you've got, making you their prime target."

Tim followed Quigley's instructions for the morning race. Careful pacing and shrewd awareness of his competitors' locations throughout the race enabled him to finish a comfortable third.

Gina on the other hand, did not win, place, or show for the first time in her athletic life. As she'd expected, the two German women were superior, and so were two other competitors. Gina's preoccupation with her father's declining health and growing concerns about her future siphoned off her competitive fire. She was relieved to have it all behind her.

###

After the morning race, Tim hydrated, relaxed, and even dozed in the shade of two large pine trees during his four-hour interim between races. Thirty minutes before his afternoon trial, feeling woolly-headed, he began a heat-abbreviated version of his usual warm-up routine—stretching and jogging followed by several moderately paced wind sprints.

But his mind was not fully present. He saw Gina sitting in the stands, and they waved to each other. Seeing her embrace her senile father the other night had touched Tim deeply. It had refreshed his desire to be back home with *his* parents. Random images flashed before him: his mother hugging him every morning, calling him her "beamish boy"; his father curling his strong, sweaty arm over Tim's shoulder after a day in the field; Millie pacing him across the hills and meadows before the sun set; herring gulls and razor bills soaring above the ocean's waters but below his dangling legs as he sat on the edge of a Mullaghmore cliff on a hot, sunny day.

The starter's announcement calling the eight-hundred-meter runners to the line startled Tim. He wasn't where he needed to be mentally—in the crucible of the racing moment. The starter's instructions brushed the outer edge of his consciousness as he stood in a fog on the starting line. Only the report of the pistol fully awakened Tim to the moment, but he got a lag start, and quickly found himself at the back of the pack—a bad situation given this level of competition.

Dumbfounded, Quigley muttered, "What the Hell!"

And when Tim hit the two-hundred-meter mark still in last place, Blake shouted, "Open your stride, Tim. Wake up! For Christ's sake! Get strong!"

Tim realized he had never run from this far behind in major competition. He knew he would have to adapt, and now.

Rather than save something for a finishing kick, Tim would

have to run "open throttle" for the remaining six hundred meters of the race. Remembering his anchor leg in the Iona Relays, Tim charged ahead, passing one runner after another. When he reached the six-hundred-meter mark, he was in third place.

Blake shouted to Tim, "Let her rip!" Tim heard the scream, but he struggled to surge. He had exhausted his reserves. His legs were moving, but they were sapped of their energy. Quigley shouted maniacally as Tim charged the finish line. He was holding pace, but he couldn't gain on the two frontrunners. The runner behind him was closing fast.

But not fast enough. Tim held on to third place by a whisker. Still, it was enough to qualify for the Championship.

On the drive back from New Haven, Quigley told Tim, Gina, and Blake that he had some exciting news for the three of them, news that he was reserving for after the track meet. He told them he'd had a call the previous night from the athletic director at Villanova University in Philadelphia. They'd offered him the head coaching job "with an excellent salary and wonderful benefits."

"Linda was hesitant at first, till she heard the terms. She's on board now, gratefully," said Quigley, nodding to his wife. "They have always had a fine track program, and the athletic director gave me ten scholarships to offer. This is where the three of you come in. Tim, Gina, and Blake. How does tuition, room, and board for four years at Villanova sound to each of you?"

Quigley expected all three to be excited by the prospect and the offer.

Tim said he liked the idea, but he wasn't sure he could make any kind of commitment until he knew what was happening with his father and mother. Blake appreciated the offer but mentioned that he was almost certainly heading west, to USC. He wanted to get as far away from St. Jude's, his family, and the East Coast as he possibly could, and as fast as possible. Tim expected Gina might accept the offer if it turned out they could continue their friendship through college. Instead, she was silent for a few moments and told Quigley she would have to think about it overnight. She looked at Tim and quietly shook her head, giving his hand a squeeze.

"We'll talk about this tomorrow," she whispered.

"Let's talk later, tonight, after we get home," he whispered, upset. "I'll have a tough time waiting till tomorrow."

Tim and Gina were silent for the remainder of the two-hour trip. Quigley, however, took the various responses in stride and was, in fact, blissfully unaware of the melodrama among his runners as he rhapsodized about his new world—the spacious campus, the variety of academic programs, the elaborate workout facilities. He even mentioned, for Tim's sake, the long tradition of championship Irish runners who'd attended Villanova—runners like Ron Delany, Eamonn Coughlin, Marcus O'Sullivan, and John Hartnett.

Chapter Fifty-Eight

TERENCE HAD HAD NOTHING TO EAT for two days now. For water, he sipped morning dew from oak or hickory leaves, and he cupped his hands to capture raindrops when the skies allowed. He knew, however, that he would not last long on the run without food and more water.

He had studiously avoided homes, traversing as much as possible the sparsely populated rural areas and back roads. He now realized that he would have to break into a home to get something to eat and drink.

After canvassing several neighborhoods for a soft target, he found an isolated home on a cul de sac a kilometer or two off Gifford Road, just south of Ballynagarrick. From behind thick, high weeds, knee-deep in a patch of yellow coltsfoot, he watched the house for more than an hour. Detecting no signs of activity, he went to the back of the house, scaled a four-foot stone wall, then approached the back window. He didn't see or hear anything, so he tried the back door. It was locked. He returned to the window and shattered it with the butt of his pistol. After reaching in to unlock the window, he slid it up and entered.

Terence went directly to the kitchen, opened the refrigerator, picked up a bottle of milk, and took deep draughts. He found some cheese and started chewing ferociously. Just as he was reaching for some cooked meat, he heard a sound behind him. He jumped, startled.

It was an old woman in her housecoat and slippers, staring at him but seemingly unconcerned with his presence.

"Are ye here to fix the fridge?" she asked.

Terence relaxed, quickly realizing that the old woman was senile.

He said, "Well, yes Missus, I'm looking at it and everything looks just fine. It may have a bit too much food, however, so I'll just take some items out of here." As Terence uttered the words, he was stuffing his pockets with some more cheese and a few cooked bangers. "Is your husband home, Missus? So I can give him my report?" he asked.

"Oh, no, my lord, no. He's long dead. Just Sonny, and he's taking a nap." At that moment, Sonny appeared draped in an open robe and rubbing his eyes. He was alarmed when he saw Terence.

"What's up, here, Officer? Something wrong?" he asked.

"Not that I found, Sonny." Terence quickly changed his story. "I was patrolling the area and saw a strange man jumping fences in the neighborhood and suspected a thief. I saw a broken window here and thought there might be a problem, but no." Terence forced a laugh. "Just a fridge that needs repair."

"This man was nice enough to help us with the refrigerator. He said it just had too much food in it," she said, and laughed.

"What's really going on here?" said Sonny. "Who the hell are ye? Ye ain't really a copper." He started to move toward Terence. Terence held up his left hand, his cocked pistol held lowered in his right.

"Ye'r right, Sonny," said Terence. "I'm a Sligo farmer and an innocent man who was wrongly arrested and thrown in H-Block. I am one of the escapees ye may have heard about. I'm on the run, and I am not going back to jail. Ye can be sure I will not hurt either of ye. I just need to be on my way. Now, I can tie ye up and gag ye, or ye can give me your word that ye will not contact the police, at least for an hour anyway."

Sonny shook his head, as though he still couldn't believe this was happening.

"Shite," he said. "Ye can be on yer way and trust me not to notify anyone. I'm no IRA guy, but I'm no Unionist either. This killin' back and forth in this country is insane. Get ye gone, and Godspeed."

"Thanks to ye both. Ye may have saved me life," said Terence, and he left by the back door.

As soon as he was gone, Sonny went to the parlor and called the police.

Chapter Fifty-Nine

AFTER FINISHING HIS SCRAPS OF FOOD and navigating off-road throughout the rainy day, Terence sought refuge for a few hours in a muddy ditch before once more testing the darkness of the main road. His primitive accommodations were beginning to wear on his nerves and his body. Incidental contact with a nettles bush while defecating in an open field had caused a painful rash on his back and buttocks. With the addition of multiple insect bites on his neck, arms, and legs, Terence was feeling more like a wild beast than a man.

Once back on the road, he walked and jogged intermittently for several tense hours before the previous day's fatigue repossessed him. Several times, he darted behind a tree or thick brush to avoid oncoming headlights. But insufficient food and constant movement were again sapping Terence's energy and alertness, causing him to react slowly to a military vehicle that came suddenly upon him, blue lights flashing and siren whooping. The vehicle's headlights and a blinding searchlight shone on his limp, weary body, and a voice from the Land Rover's loudspeaker instructed him to raise his hands and drop to his knees. Terence did neither. Exhausted and desolate, he drew his pistol and fired several shots at the Rover, shattering the lights and wounding a soldier. He tossed his empty pistol and began running again, this time running faster than he had ever run before—long, desperate strides seeking distance between him and the Rover.

Soon after tending to his lightly wounded partner, the driver switched on the two roof searchlights and resumed his pursuit.

Terence felt the Rover closing on him. At the same time, he spotted a vehicle speeding at him from the opposite direction. Terence thought he was finished. He would either be killed here or sent back to prison. The approaching vehicle, however, passed him and swerved violently into the lane of the oncoming Rover, forcing it to a tire-screeching halt. Suddenly, an AK-47 poked out of the back window and sprayed a dozen or more bullets into the Rover.

The only noise for a moment was the hissing of its punctured radiator. Then an old man's voice bellowed from the mystery automobile.

"You! Get in here. Hurry!"

Chapter Sixty

TIM FOUND GINA WAITING FOR HIM on her front porch. She greeted him with a tearful smile and a warm embrace. He was about to say something, but she gently placed her two fingers on his lips.

"No, not yet. Let me say my piece, so I can get it out. I've been rehearsing this stuff all evening." She took a deep breath. "First, let's be clear. You ain't a greenhorn or goofball anymore, are you? You're the real deal now, and I am happy for you. I'm really, really proud of you."

Tim felt a shock of sadness, sensing that she was about to change their relationship. He was right.

She put her arms around Tim and said there were "a bunch of reasons" why the time was right for him and for her, but not for *them*. They would be traveling different paths from now on. He would be moving on to college to get a diploma and become a famous runner. She wouldn't be going to college, even with a track scholarship. At least for some time, anyway. She explained that she was sick of school and needed to work and earn some money. Also, she was tired of the constant training and the competition, saying she had enjoyed all the victories and the "hoorahs," but she did it mainly to blow off steam. More to the main point, she knew that she and Tim were too young to get serious, and there was always the real possibility that Tim would return to Ireland. She was pretty sure a fishing village in rural Ireland was not the place for a foul-mouthed, six-foot Italian American girl from Queens, NY.

She also told Tim, in all seriousness, that now that they had cracked the virginity code, she'd be all over him, "wearing him down so bad he would have trouble walking, never mind running. And what if she got pregnant?"

Most of all, she couldn't leave her sick father.

Tim nodded sadly. "I know."

Gina took his face in her hands. "You're on your way now, Tim. I predict wonderful things for you. And for me too, actually. We'll be fine. Just not together. At least not now." She paused and choked up. "In spite of all this, dear Tim, I love you, and I am going to miss you something terrible."

Tim tried to speak but could not. Instead, he embraced Gina, and they sobbed into one another's shoulders. When he could speak, Tim said that Gina was his first true friend in America and his first ever lover. She said he was not only her first ever lover . . . he was her first ever friend anywhere. They swore to be friends forever and determined to spend their time together until he went off to college.

Chapter Sixty-One

ONCE TERENCE WAS SECURE IN THE BACKSEAT, the car sped off in the direction it came from. The driver told Terence that they were an IRA recon team searching for H-Block escapees. They had spotted him the night before as they were patrolling the area, but the guard's uniform had thrown them off.

"We learned from another escapee we picked up last night," the driver said, "that some of ye were disguised as guards, so we decided to patrol this night too. Ye looked like a drowned dog in that filthy uniform, so we figured ye were not a real copper, and when we saw that Land Rover chasing you, the old codger in the back seat with the AK-47 told me to cut them off. That's when he unloaded on them."

Terence, teetering between shock and fatigue, labored to speak.

"Many thanks to ye, sir, to all of ye for saving me life. Terence Connolly's me name."

"Well, I'll be damned, son. Mike Scully's me name. Ye can thank Larry Flynn here for trackin' ye down. He knows these roads like the veins in his hand, and he can still do some fancy driving. And by the way, boyo, I believe we have a surprise comin' your way."

Months after these events, Larry Flynn rented a room near Scully in Sligo. His long-suffering wife had recently died, and his children had long ago left Ireland. His son had taken an engineering job in Germany, and his daughter and her children moved to England to escape her abusive husband, since divorce was illegal in Ireland.

Flynn sought the company of the shrinking number of people who knew his history, who knew his few amiable qualities, and who could also tolerate his sudden episodes of volatile behavior. Predictably, several weeks after his arrival, he and Scully were savoring their pints at McGovern's and rehashing the previous year's wild adventures when Flynn objected to a young customer's loud and disagreeable opinions about Sligo's football team. He told the customer to "shut the hell up."

The young fella replied, "Fuck off, ye old bugger!"

Flynn never liked being told to "fuck off"—or to "go fuck himself," for that matter. This occasion was no different. But being called "an old bugger" in the bargain was an outrage he would not endure. Forgetting his age, Flynn took a deep breath, staggered forward, and shakily raised his bony fist to strike the amused and unrattled customer.

At that very moment, Flynn suffered a massive stroke and died on the spot.

Scully managed the funeral arrangements, and delivered a moving and, at the same time, wildly funny eulogy at Flynn's funeral mass. He later entertained the funeral party at McGovern's with a string of Flynn stories from the distant past—highlighted, of course, by his unhinged, two-gun "Pancho Villa" assault on the British platoon in '21.

Chapter Sixty-Two

After a twenty-minute ride, they arrived at a safe house in Armagh. The house was one of several south of Milford, set off the road in an excavated lot surrounded by a thick canopy of beech and sycamore trees.

When Terence walked in, he immediately noticed an old man with a crutch bent over a table, scanning a map with a compass. Terence shouted.

"Brian Connolly! Grandfather!"

Brian looked up from his map and beamed when he saw his grandson. He grabbed him, shook him, and kissed his cheek.

"Jaysus, Terence, I was *hoping* ye would be one of the lads who escaped. Jaysus, it's so good to see ye in one piece, lad."

Terence, dizzy with exhaustion, could only say, "Brian, ye ancient rebel! How the hell are ye here?"

"Let's get ye a hot whiskey before we find a bed and some clean clothes for ye, and I'll tell ye the short tale." Brian escorted his weary grandson to a plush armchair, handed him a hot drink, and began explaining how, why, and when he was released from H-Block. His physical breakdown, he told Terence, was real—the product of some robust thrashing from a couple of guards.

"In truth, I spiced the thumping with some wailing theatrics," he said, "to make the bastards think I was near death. So, they released me." While Brian was warming to his tale of derring-do, he failed to notice that Terence's head was lolling from side to side.

Oblivious, he continued, telling Terence how he joined forces with the IRA. "At first they welcomed us . . ."

Brian paused a moment as he finally saw Terence nodding off. He coughed loud enough to open his grandson's eyes, then continued, "But . . . we, ah, volunteered to do patrols searching for escapees on the run."

Finally, he saw the futility of continuing. Terence was asleep and snoring, He shook Terence gently, this time to share good news. "One more thing before we find ye a bed, lad. We've been in touch with Bridget. I told her that since ye were hunger striking, and as she was publicly agitating against Belfast's abuses, the IRA would tap into its family fund to help her with her expenses. She has been a godsend, son. And sure, won't ye be amazed when I tell ye what she's done? And she . . . she will be ecstatic when we get word about you to her tomorrow."

Terence, half asleep, said, "I need to talk with her now."

No phones just yet," said Brian. "The RUC and the Loyalists have their eyes and ears on her now, but we'll have a plan by morning. Right now, ye need to rest."

Chapter Sixty-Three

THE EVENING TRAIN FROM DUBLIN took several hours. While Bridget slept, Maeve skimmed through a stack of newspapers and current magazines, searching for information that might be useful to them. At the Sligo rail station, they picked up Maeve's car and headed toward Mullaghmore. Bridget took the wheel after Maeve nodded off and almost drove into a ditch.

When she finally arrived at the gravel road leading to her cottage, Bridget slowed, then stopped the car.

"Oh my God," she murmured breathlessly.

"What's the matter?" Maeve asked, startled.

"Maeve! My car is on fire! And the lights are on in the cottage. There are two cars outside, and I hear voices. What should we do?"

Maeve said, "Let's get the hell out of here."

Bridget froze behind the wheel.

Startled by the lights in the driveway, six men dashed from the cottage and jumped into their cars. They began shouting and screaming when they saw Maeve's car. Suddenly, two cars accelerated and headed straight toward them. Maeve and Bridget panicked. They covered and lowered their heads as the speeding cars swerved by them. The first car fired several shots in the air. The second car fired at the car as they sped past. One bullet hit the boot of Maeve's car. The cars sped wildly off the farm and down the road.

"O my God, Maeve, O my God!" Bridget screamed.

"This is bad. Let's check the house and see what they did." said Maeve. "We'll call the police from your house."

Bridget stopped the car thirty meters from the burning car and the entrance to the cottage. She started to tremble. What she saw when she stepped out of the car filled her with horror and revulsion.

Three of her sheep and two cows had been shot and crudely slaughtered near the front door. Beyond them was the bleeding carcass of the Connollys' trusted, beloved, hard-working donkey, Zeus. Bridget's legs went weak. She staggered to the boot of the car, braced herself on the rear fender and vomited.

Maeve approached the cottage and noticed the walls were spray painted with graffiti: "Welcome Home, IRA whore." "Your time is up, Fenian bitch." "Run or die!" She opened the front door and surveyed the house. The furniture was thrown about the house, most of it shattered. Strewn on the floor were the entrails of the slaughtered animals.

"These dirty fuckers!" shouted Maeve. "They won't get away with this." She paused. "Looks like a note on your door." She removed it. "Oh, these bastards . . ." She caught her breath. "It says if their people 'ever see hide or hare of you here again, they will burn your house to the ground with you in it.'"

"Oh my God, Maeve. Let's get out of here," Bridget said after wiping off her mouth.

"'*Hare*!" Maeve, distracted, was still gazing at the note, and whispered to herself, "Stupid bastards. Vicious and stupid."

"Let's get out of here, Maeve. Let me stay with ye tonight, please, till I can figure out what to do."

"Absolutely, my dear."

Chapter Sixty-Four

THE NEXT MORNING, MAEVE'S HUSBAND, Joe, made breakfast for his wife and a badly shaken Bridget. She hadn't slept all night and had no appetite. She nixed the porridge and eggs. She took one bite of her toast and slowly sipped her tea. Maeve reported the incident to the local Gardai, who went to the Connolly home, inspected it, removed the dead livestock, and cleared the offal from the house. One of the marauders had defecated in the kitchen. Other than that, Inspector Feherty reported that they could find no useful clues, but they would keep their eyes open.

"They'll keep their feckin eyes open," Maeve sneered. "Eyes open? Find clues? These eejits couldn't find their own arses if they each had ten arms. Chubby Chief Inspector Feherty—isn't he of course the least of the group? That big tub of guts struts around town like he's General Michael Collins. More like Fatty feckin Arbuckle. He couldn't solve a two-piece crossword puzzle if ye gave him an entire month. Sure, and he's forever flirting with the widows and the spinsters, waddling about town, sportin' his badge and twirlin' his bloody nightstick. I've never known a one to give him the time of day. Ach . . . he's been a lickarse ever since grade school. Keep their eyes open . . . bollocks . . . "

"I have an idea," interjected Bridget, inattentive to Maeve's monologue. "Let's call Avery Donnellon and see if he can help?"

With that, Bridget and Maeve spent several hours tracking

down Donnellon, leaving messages with his various associates. When he finally returned their call, he listened intently to Maeve's description of the events. He told her he would have some of his local people investigate and track down the "bloody cowards" who did it.

"In the meantime," Donnellon said, "I've some good news for ye."

"Jaysus," said Maeve. "We sure could use some."

"Put Bridget on the phone please, Maeve," he said.

Maeve handed her the phone.

"Bridget, here," she said.

"Bridget, your Terence is free. He was one of the escaped prisoners, and he's found his way to one of our safe houses."

"Oh my God!" she screamed. "Terence's escaped." Bridget handed the phone to Maeve and walked aimlessly around the living room, clutching her hair, laughing while crying. "Oh my God, he's free," she repeated. "He's free! Let me have the phone again, Maeve, please."

Taking it, she asked, "When can I see him?"

"Very soon, Mrs. Connolly," Donnellon replied. "We will be moving him over the border very shortly, and then we will be fixing the lad with some new identity papers, including a passport. Once we do that, we'll have a few of our people take him to a remote area in Sligo, where you can be together. We'll let you know more tomorrow. We won't tell him anything of the attack on your home until he's on his way to Sligo. We need him concentrating on getting out safely and secured with a new identity. Be assured, though, that we will seek out the villains who attacked you and your home and punish them."

Chapter Sixty-Five

SUNLIGHT FILTERED THROUGH the dirt-crusted and cracked windows of an abandoned trolley depot three blocks behind the Fresh Pond Road elevated station. Cooper and Benson were curled in sleeping bags in a dark, dirt-packed corner, hidden behind rusted tire rims, axles, and a rotted-out gearbox. Cooper stirred, sat up, and pushed Benson.

"What'd you do with that bag of food?" he asked. Benson grumbled and pointed at a broken, dust-covered scrap of sheet metal, a fender of some sort.

"Behind that thing," he said. Cooper retrieved the bag, picked up a bottle of milk, took a gulp, then spit it out.

"Aaargh . . . this shit's sour," he said. "What else we got?" He found a candy bar, tore open the wrapper, and started chewing. Benson sat up, stretched, wiped his eyes with his grimy hands.

"What the hell we gonna do next, Coop? I'm getting tired of all this. We've been on the run for weeks now, and I'm always fuckin' hungry. Besides, we can't stay cooped up in this shithole forever. Hey that's funny. Get it? Cooped up?"

Cooper raised his eyelids, shook his head, and finished munching his candy bar.

"A few more days," he said. "First, we gotta make another shoplifting run at A&P. We better be more careful this time. Hide the food more carefully. I don't wanna beat up another store manager just to get out of the store. I worry they might have some cops waiting for us next time." Cooper scratched his greasy scalp and pondered the day's activities. "Also, tell your stupid brother to leave some clean clothes for us. One other thing—make sure he hides those sweat suits for us in a black plastic bag, you know, behind the dumpster near the baseball field."

Benson stared at Cooper, expecting more.

"Yeah. Got it. Then what?"

"Unfinished business—then we can get the hell out of town" Cooper said.

"What you got in mind?" asked Benson.

"Randall's Island next week. Payback. I told that Irish prick he was a dead man, and I meant it," said Cooper as he searched the bag for more food. "I still have dear old dad's revolver hidden in my uncle's garage. I'm gonna break in there tomorrow night and get it."

"This is gettin' outta hand, Coop. I don't wanna be involved in no killin'. You almost killed Quigley. Why don't we just quit now . . . get the hell outta town, head upstate or to Jersey?

"You turnin' pussy on me, like Blake? This'll be it. I promise," said Cooper.

Chapter Sixty-Six

OVER THE NEXT FEW DAYS, NEWS SPREAD through Ireland, Britain, and Europe about the H-Block escape. Since it was the biggest prison break since WWII, it garnered headlines for a full week. During the escape, four prison officers had been stabbed; one was shot and killed. No news of the shooting on Terence's escape route had yet hit the papers.

Of the thirty-eight escapees, the RUC and British army had recaptured nineteen. Nineteen others, like Terence, had escaped into the protection of the IRA.

Unbeknownst to Terence, his prison mate, McCahill, was one of those captured. He'd been five miles from the prison, hiding underwater in a pond, breathing through a reed when he was spotted by an army patrol. He surrendered eagerly when several warning bullets splashed dangerously close to his head. Soggy, stinking, and despondent, McCahill took multiple blows to the head, back, and ribs before he was dragged back to his cell. Battered and depressed, he was buoyed nonetheless by the cheers of his once-again fellow inmates. He soon settled back into his old prison routine, but a profound emptiness infected him.

Doug McQuarrie confronted him soon after returned to his old cell.

"So ye were a bloody priest! Defrocked, no less!" said McQuarrie. "That's feckin hilarious! That's quite a leap from yer sayin a Papist Mass to blowin' people to kingdom come!"

"Well, there were multiple causes for the defrocking . . . the robberies," said McCahill defensively. "That was the main one. And the dalliances with women. They, uh, also crossed the bishop's line."

"Dalliances ye'll be callin' them now, eh?" sniped McQuarrie.

McCahill proceeded, deaf to the guard's mocking tone. "Well, yeah, and once defrocked, especially in such a public and shameful way, sure, no one would hire me, and even if they would, I had no skills." McCahill joked lamely, "No one pays defrocked priests to give sermons or to hear their confessions. Munitions seemed an easy enough skill to learn. And the IRA didn't care that I was a priest. Like you, they made a joke of it actually. So, there you have it."

"McCahill, take this any way you like," McQuarrie sneered. "But ye seem like, uh—you seem like kind of a silly man. Look at ye, ye'r an educated fella. And ye'r getting on in years. What have ye got to show for it? Ye've spent yer adult life fuckin lonely women and stealin' from yer church. Then ye set about blowin' up innocent people! For the love of God, man, why don't ye do something worthwhile with what's left of yer life while ye'r in here. Make a difference? Something like that, eh?"

Shaken by this comment, McCahill went silent. McQuarrie had touched a nerve. Of course, he *was* a silly man. Worse, a fool. A shallow aimless fool who wasted his life. The next day, he asked the guard to bring him some notebooks and ball point pens.

McCahill began writing. And writing. His words quickly filled ten notebooks. The words formed thoughts, and the thoughts turned into tales from his childhood, tales from his years as a lecherous teenager and a petty thief, one who inconceivably became a seminarian, a parish priest, and ultimately, a terrorist. *It was published as* Memoir of a Defrocked Parish Priest *and became a best-seller, savored primarily for the salacious parts dealing with sex and crime.*

It was followed by Memoir of a Political Prisoner, *which was valued more for the sordid and brutal detail of daily life in H-Block. It became an important document in the later investigations of prison conditions by government committees. These early forays in the literary world were followed by several books of mediocre poetry. His most respected work,* Suffer the Little Children, *was a scathing insider profile and indictment of the systemic child abuse in Ireland's schools, churches, and orphanages. McCahill also volunteered many of his prison hours, especially teaching writing to his fellow inmates. This activity earned him a commendation for good behavior and early release in 1991. Not long after his release, he packaged his priestly speaking skills with his writing skills and traveled the European and American lecture circuit for the next fifteen years.*

Chapter Sixty-Seven

WRAPPED IN A SLEEPING BAG on a canvas cot, Terence slept for ten hours. When he woke, he sat down to a breakfast of scrambled eggs, rashers, bangers, potatoes, and fried tomato, plus a pot of strong breakfast tea—his first decent food in months. His grandfather greeted him warmly and told him again how proud he was of him. He poured himself a cup of tea and smiled at his grandson, then placed his hand affectionately on his shoulder. Brian's demeanor took a sudden dark turn. He started to speak to Terence, then stopped and took a sip of his tea. He started to speak again, and his eyes welled with tears.

Terence was startled. He had never seen the old man like this, so he reached over and touched his hand.

"What's the matter, Grandfather?"

Brian tried to wave away the question and the need for a response, but he couldn't. "I thought I'd lost ye, Terence, and I couldn't stand the thought," he said. "If it wasn't for me, lad, ye never would have been at that border and suffered as ye did. I lost me own Michael—yer Da—for being a stubborn, thoughtless bastard. I couldn't deal with the thought of losing *his* boy as well."

Terence wasn't sure what to say. He held his grandfather's hand while the old man wept and spoke. "Yer Da was a splendid man," said Brian. "He was stubborn to a fault, like most of us Connolly's. But he had his own stern principles. He could not be pushed around, not even by me. I wanted him to be like me, an IRA man.

He was republican to the core, but he wanted no part of the violence. He just wanted to work his farm and raise his family in peace, like you, lad."

Brian stood up and lit a cigarette, shaking his head and wiping his nose with a handkerchief as he looked out the window. "But the whole family fell on hard times in the thirties, and your Da thought if he enlisted in the army, he could make money to send home. So, he joined the Canadian Army when the war started. He couldn't abide fighting with the British. At least we agreed on that. But we disagreed that fighting the Germans was anything we should get involved in. De Valera urged neutrality. I agreed with him—at first, anyway—since the Germans had always supported us against England in the past."

Brian paused to catch his breath and wipe his nose again. Terence held a solemn gaze on him. "But since we separated on bad terms, I never got a chance to set it right. It ruined me life with yer grandmother. She blamed me till the day she died. Rightly so. I was no comfort to her. Me silent response to Michael's death contributed to Moira's despair and her suicide. And yer Ma, yer Ma . . . God bless her. When yer Da came home in that box, well . . . it was a dark day for all of us, but too much for her. She loved him deeply and depended on him completely. Too much so."

Brian paused to catch his breath.

"I was too young to remember that day," said Terence. "I know she had a tough time managing our farm and me, but her sister, Lilian, Aunt Lilian and her husband Devin, helped her with chores and helped raise me."

"Two weeks ago," Brian blurted, "I woke from a dream calling

Michael's name, asking him to forgive me. I thought I saw his face in my bedroom mirror."

Terence seemed helpless to allay his grandfather's deepening sadness. He attempted to rally him with reassurances of the good he *had* done with his life, how he served his country with courage and devotion, how he became a surrogate father to *him* and a magical friend to Tim. When Brian pursed his lips and shook his head, resisting the slightest shred of consolation, Terence placed his hand gently on his grandfather's bald head.

This touch released a torrent of tears.

After a few moments, Brian wiped his eyes with his sleeve, wiped his nose again, then took a sip of his tea, his hand shaking.

"At any rate, Terence, me lad," the old man began haltingly, "I think I can help ye and yer family now. We are getting ye a new name and a passport. We are going to get ye back with Bridget and Tim, and then set ye up with a job and a home in America."

"Thank ye, Brian. I'm happy to hear that. I've had enough of this bloody mayhem. I'm just a farmer, as ye well know. That and me wife and me boy are all that I ever wanted. I'm grateful to ye, old man."

Chapter Sixty-Eight

THE NEXT DAY, BRIAN LAID OUT another map that Flynn had color coded for his grandson. Brian knew the Army and RUC would be patrolling the main route from Armagh to Monahan, and they would have to pass through numerous checkpoints. Still, winding strands of country roads circled and crisscrossed the main roads toward and around Keady in the direction of Carnagh Forest Park. These alternate roads featured several safehouses if needed. From the Park, heavily forested woods led to a sparsely inhabited but still guarded section of the border not too far from where the IRA had dug escape tunnels under the Cor River border.

"We'll drop ye on this side of the border," Brian said, "then we'll drive across the border checkpoint and pick ye up on the other side of Monaghan Road." Brian showed his grandson the map. "This route will get us out of here in fine fettle."

Terence raised his eyebrows. "Us?"

"Yes indeed, lad. I thought about it some last night after we spoke. I've had a lifetime of all this. Enough is enough. Me and me boyos. This is it. Scully's drivin' ahead to spot the roadblocks, and he'll radio the locations to us. They'll get us as close to the border as possible, let ye out near the tunnel where some of our lads should be waiting for ye, and we'll meet ye on the other side. We're taking ye back to Bridget, and we're going to fix things right. Then . . . then we'll be done."

Terence laughed. He was about to speak, but instead, he

grappled the old man and kissed his hairy cheek.

The trip down Monaghan Road went smoothly until they approached the border where, as expected, Army troops were stopping every car, opening boots, and checking undercarriages and IDs. Scully radioed back to Brian to drop Terence at Mackle's Ice Cream shop, three kilometers before the border.

"Tell him," Scully said, "to cross the road and head two kilometers due southeast along the hedgerow bordering the open pasture. When he sees the Devaney Memorial, he'll find a sewer plate to the tunnel about twenty-five meters behind the memorial. There may or may not be someone there to help him. Under the cover, stone steps lead into the tunnel that runs under the River Cor. When he gets out, tell him that we'll meet him at the petrol station on R213, about 250 meters from the tunnel. Ditch the radios before ye get to the border."

The plan worked. Terence ran carefully along the hedgerow. After about half an hour, he found the Devaney Memorial. He lifted the sewer plate and crawled into the dank and foul-smelling tunnel. Terence wasn't claustrophobic, but this was different. The tubular enclosure was thick with mud, rotted leaves, spider webs, sewage, and rats scurrying past his face. Once he emerged, he felt as if he had passed through the bowels of a whale. He walked slowly to the petrol station and settled in the back seat of the waiting car, wet, muddy, and ungodly ripe.

"Mother o' God," said Brian, finger to his nose. "Ye smell like a feckin' shithouse. Ye'r bloody safe now. No copper with a sense of smell would ever get close enough to arrest ye." After cracking open a window, Brian explained that they would first drive to Carrick-on-Shannon to meet the IRA contractor who forged Terence's passport. After that, they would drive the final fifty kilometers to Coolaney. Brian told Terence that Bridget would meet him there at the Mountain Inn. Terence longed to see his home but sadly agreed it would be better to avoid being seen in Mullaghmore.

Brian did not tell Terence about the desecration of his home and property, the gunshots, and the death threats to Bridget. Better to let him spend some time with Bridget first. Perhaps she'd break the news.

Forty-five kilometers south of Terence's farm, the Mountain Inn was nestled into the Ox Mountains, a scenic area where Terence and Bridget had spent time hiking and biking the surrounding trails when they were younger. The location provided the relative privacy and security they required, not only to be hidden from public view but also to become reacquainted with each other. Though Terence and Bridget felt the pain of every hour separated from each other for so long, the separation had changed them. Bridget had unexpectedly crafted a new identity out of her loss. She was now more than the loving wife and mother, more than a helpmate in their working farm. She had discovered an independent voice and an unexpected assertive power. Terence himself had changed from a hard-working, introverted, and friendly neighbor into a bitter man fueled with a righteous anger.

He'd never realized, until recent months, how hatred could consume a man and feed the desire to inflict pain on his enemy. And kill him, if necessary. How their changes might affect their reacquaintance worried Bridget more than Tim.

On the trip to Coolaney, Brian detailed the extent of Bridget's activities on his behalf and that of the other prisoners in H-Block. He produced press clippings to give him a sense of her effectiveness in producing results along with her partner, Maeve Grogan.

"Truly, I am not surprised," Terence gushed. "Her lovely face has always hidden a will of steel. When she puts her mind to something, sure, she is a force to be reckoned with, as I well know. Team her with Maeve Grogan, and I'm sure they would give bloody Thatcher and her whole cabinet of twats a run for their money." Brian nodded quietly and murmured affirmation but said nothing of the threats and the attack on their home as a result of her anti-H-Block crusade.

Chapter Sixty-Nine

BRIDGET WAS WAITING OUTSIDE THE MOUNTAIN Inn when the two cars arrived at 11 a.m.

When Terence stepped out, Bridget walked slowly to him. She needed to calm her racing imagination and throbbing pulse to assure herself that this moment was real. Terence was here, and the awful time without him had ended.

Conscious of his battered and worn condition, Terence wondered if Bridget might somehow be disappointed at the sight of him. Might his damaged appearance diminish him in her eyes? Standing face-to-face, they looked sadly into each other's eyes. Then they gently touched each other's faces, embraced gingerly, and trembled before clumsily kissing each other's tear-soaked cheeks and lips.

Bridget pulled back from her husband, laughing and with tears in her eyes.

"Oh Terence," she said. "I've missed ye so much. Welcome home, me love." She hugged him and kissed him again, then pulled back again, laughing. "I have no idea where ye have been spending yer time, dear man, but Jaysus, Mary, and Joseph, we have to do something with ye. Ye look like hell and smell like a manure pile. Let's get ye inside, get ye a hot bath and a shave, and we'll have us a nice lie down." Terence's fears and uncertainties dissipated in that moment, redeemed in himself and in them.

"Bridget, me love," he said with a smile, "ye have grown more beautiful as I have grown more beastly. I think we have a story here."

After taking Bridget's hand in his, Terence told Brian that they would meet him for dinner. They went to their room. He shaved, and they showered. Then they navigated each other's naked bodies with unreserved relish for a few hours until sleep overtook them.

When they awoke, Bridget recounted her political activities with Maeve, their meetings with dignitaries, and their notorious newspaper and television experiences. She saved the worst for last, tentatively explaining to Terence how their notoriety created enemies, even violent ones. She nervously told him of their slaughtered animals, the destroyed car, the defilement of their home, and the threats to her life.

Terence was, at first, incredulous, sympathetic, and dumbfounded. Then he lost control. Bridget had known he would be angry, but she hadn't expected the spitting, fist-waving rage that overtook him. He ranted in a fury, cursing to hell the terrorists that had attacked his wife and home. When would it end? First, they fractured his family, separating father, mother, and son. Imprisoning him. And for what? For nothing. For fucking lies! And now this? This would not stand. The very nature of the deed cried for blood.

Bridget attempted at first to quell his anger but soon realized that Terence would not be comforted. He stormed out of their room, down the stairs to the bar where Brian, Scully, and Flynn waited. They knew he would be upset, and they braced for his reaction. They were not disappointed.

"So, ye all knew of this," Terence shouted.

"We knew ye'd find out soon enough, lad. We didn't want to

spoil yer first hours with yer wife. Nothing could have been done by us anyway," said Brian.

Terence continued his profane outburst against the threats to wife and the damage to his property. His anger ripped the scab off the simmering humiliations and the physical and emotional pain he had endured for months in H-Block.

Minutes later, Bridget entered the pub just as Terence, swearing revenge, smacked his hand violently on the bar, causing glasses to jump and topple. The disturbance startled the few customers in the pub. Brian gestured to Scully and Flynn to get rid of the customers, mostly for their own safety. Terence was inconsolable. Bridget signaled to Brian to let him express his rage, hoping he would calm himself.

When Terence paused for a moment to catch his breath, Brian spoke softly, attempting to reassure his grandson that the matter was "well in hand."

"Well in hand, me arse," said Terence, shaking his head in surly repudiation. "No! No, Grandfather. Nothing without me"

"I understand the depth of yer anger, son. Believe me, I have eaten revenge for breakfast almost every day of me life. You will get yours, as God is me witness. But ye will not be the avenging angel. No, not this time. And for one reason: the wheels are already in motion. A few IRA boyos and one very violent woman are already setting a trap for the villains who fouled your home and threatened Bridget's life. They will be very surprised and very dead assassins when they make their next visit."

Terence, still tense with outrage, red-eyed and sweating, was thrown off guard by this unexpected news. He welcomed the idea of speedy revenge, but he felt put off that he would not be the agent of the vengeance.

As he assessed this new revelation, Bridget stood next to him and took his hand. She could feel it soften in hers. Then she grabbed Terence's face and pressed her forehead to his, hoping her touch and her words might reach him.

"Terence, me love, why do ye think I've been working day after day with Maeve and our women's crusade? Why do ye think yer grandfather and his lads were working with the IRA? It was to get ye out of prison, so ye could come back to me, so you could see the son who loves and misses ye desperately. Think about *now*. Think *tomorrow*, me dear man. The past year has been a bloody mess. We can change it. We are going to change it."

Terence's rage ebbed, and he pulled Bridget to him.

"Ye'r right, of course, me darlin'. I am sorry. The thought of someone doin' harm to ye makes me crazy, and after all they've done to us, to our family. But . . . I'm all right. I'll be okay now. At least I hope so." He grinned. "And sure, seeing Tim should pull the broken pieces together, eh?"

Knowing that the terrorists would be punished satisfied Terence. Knowing that he would soon be reunited with his son inspired him with hope, or as much hope as he could muster in his present state.

Though nervous, Bridget, in truth, felt much the same way. If their last journey into the unknown had brought them unexpected chaos and grief, maybe this journey would be different. Better. They hoped.

"So . . ." Brian started, "ye have yer new passport, and the three of us will be off to America tomorrow. Maeve has packed your necessities and she'll be driving us to Shannon. "Yer brother-in-law, Mr. Gary Laherty, has an apartment and a temporary job waiting for ye in Queens, New York, and most of all, young Tim Connolly, yer young fella and me great-grandson is in for the surprise of his life when he gets to see his ma and his Da tomorrow. By the way, he has apparently become quite the young man."

"As for yer home, Maeve will look after it," said Scully. "She plans to operate the cottage as a B&B to cover expenses till these troubles end and ye can return home. Her two boys plan to populate the farm with some new animals and tend the farming chores. And sure, I'll be helping with the maintaining of yer home."

###

Weeks later, Scully moved to Mullaghmore, where he rented a room above McGovern's Pub. He reconnected with a few old acquaintances, whom he would meet weekly for pints and craic. As promised, he worked part-time for Maeve Grogan, assisting her and her sons with the upkeep of the Connolly farm. Her sons managed the fields and the livestock. Scully minded the Connolly cottage for two tourist seasons. He took care of the hoovering, scrubbing, and mopping, and making sure there was an adequate supply of clean sheets, soap, towels, and toilet tissue. He inhabited the cottage during the off-season months, keeping the place clean and secure.

He soon grew accustomed to the solitary life. Scully's wife had died twenty-two years earlier, and he'd never remarried. He had no children, and his few companions were the men he knew from McGovern's or those he met through Liam Daley, the Turf Accountant. He grew to cherish his winter isolation, believing the silence was heightening his perceptions of things, even the simplest of things. He delighted in the firelight and heat radiating from the hearth, mocking and thwarting the thrashing winter wind and rain that assailed the thick walls of the cottage. The crackling nightly fire and its complex scent of burning peat and cherry wood became, for him, the purest earthly pleasure.

This monastic existence opened a door one night to Scully's past. Half asleep in front of the fire's glowing embers, Scully unexpectedly began mumbling disjointed Latin phrases from his youth as an altar boy, phrases he hadn't uttered in over sixty years: Ad Deum qui laetificat juventutum meum . . . Confetior dei omnipotenti . . . mea culpa, mea culpa, mea maxima culpa . . . Kyrie eleiason, Christe eleiason . . . Dominun vobiscum, Et cum spiritu tuo.

Shards and splinters of religious chaff cracked and floated up from archives of a distant youth that had once been cemented in faith. Stirring his tea another night, words from an old prayer book tumbled into his mind: "Lord I am not worthy that Thou shouldst come unto me; speak but the word, and my soul shall be healed."

Scully sought to quell this intrusive babble, wondering what the hell was going on. He felt somehow possessed. Divine possession? These repeated Latin and English pieties visited him for successive nights, mysteriously seeping out of his mind's sanctuary like wine from a cracked chalice. Strange stuff, Scully mused, since within three years of serving at Mass, he had eagerly abandoned and rejected the coercive power of the church and had taken arms against his enemies. And he never forgave, and he never turned the other cheek. He chose, instead, to maim and kill—with gusto and without guilt. The British spies he took off the train and shot in the back of the head in '21 bothered him not a whit, though the praying afterward did.

These fitful visits subsided after several weeks, finally allowing him to sleep peacefully through the night.

After one such peaceful night, Scully did not waken. When his cold, gray body was discovered in his bed after several days, Maeve's boys collected and boxed his meager belongings, among them two items from his bedstead: a sepia photo of four young, grinning soldiers from the war—Scully, Flynn, Brian, and Brian's brother Tim—and a small, porcelain statue of the Virgin Mary ensnared in a desiccated rosary with a rusted crucifix and a dozen or more missing wooden beads.

Chapter Seventy

TWO NIGHTS EARLIER, THREE IRA MEN and one woman had moved into the Connolly cottage. During the day, the woman made herself visible with outdoor chores—hanging out laundry, tending her garden, beating carpets, and walking about with a Millie lookalike. The men only left the house for short breaks at night. The windows on either end of the cottage became firing positions for two men. Each night, the third man unfolded a beach chair, wrapped himself in a camouflage tarp, and positioned himself behind a large walnut tree near the driveway entrance. Two hundred meters from the cottage, he was equipped with a Kalashnikov automatic rifle, a pistol, and a two-way radio to announce any "guests."

After two days of staging, the plan worked. These would-be assassins were, as Maeve surmised, "stupid as well as vicious." Shortly after nightfall, two cars drove into the trap. They parked their cars some distance from the house, not far from the IRA man behind the walnut tree. They jogged quietly to the cottage, pistols and a large can of petrol in hand, planning to surprise "Bridget" and torch the cottage. The man behind the tree calmly radioed the men and woman in the house that the assassins had arrived. When six of them approached the front door, they were met by a fusillade of bullets from the two windows. The woman appeared from the far end of the cottage trapping them in a withering crossfire.

Four assailants fell immediately. The two survivors bolted,

sprinting helter-skelter toward their car, only to be interrupted and shot repeatedly by the third IRA man. The six bodies were tossed three in the boot of each vehicle and driven north to Donegal, then parked on a remote dirt road two miles from the Northern Ireland border. A third car, driven by "Bridget," picked up the IRA drivers and took them back to Mullaghmore for a steak dinner.

Chapter Seventy-One

TERENCE, BRIDGET, AND BRIAN were scheduled to depart Shannon at 2 p.m. on July 9. They would land at Kennedy around 3:30 EST. Brian told Terence that he had sent a telegram to Gary Laherty, letting him and Mary know when their plane would arrive.

Gary had responded that July 9 was a big day for the family—Tim was competing in a national championship race. Gary knew their flight would arrive too late for them to attend the race, but he was arranging a "Win or Lose Celebration"—an Irish "Trad Session"—for family and friends for the evening after the race, and he hoped they might arrive in time to surprise Tim.

"That sounds wonderful," said Terence. "Maybe we can arrange something special for the lad."

Bridget smiled. "Yes, absolutely."

Early on the morning of July 9, Maeve delivered Terence's and Bridget's suitcases, then drove them and Brian the two hundred kilometers to Shannon Airport to catch their afternoon flight to Kennedy. Maeve spent most of the trip to the airport expressing her sorrow over her friends' departure. She promised that she and her boys would take good care of Millie and the farm, and she would let them know about the latest happenings in

Mullaghmore. Maeve also mentioned that she had formed a committee that had hired a Sligo law firm to clear Terence's record, restore his good name, and make it possible for the family to return to their farm as soon as possible. Terence, Bridget, and Brian comprehended only a fraction of what Maeve was saying since she was driving at dangerously high speeds while constantly twisting to maintain eye contact with her three passengers. Brian several times pleaded with her to keep her eyes on the road but to no avail. Terence later confessed, half joking, that the trip to Shannon was more terrifying than anything he experienced in H-Block. When they arrived at the airport, Bridget embraced Maeve and thanked her for her many kindnesses.

"I know I couldn't have made it without your strength and support, me dear Maeve. God must have sent you to me," said Bridget.

"Forget the God stuff, me love. Ye have become me dearest friend, and I will miss ye enormously. I was proud to work beside ye, and ye simply astonished me with the grace and power ye brought to our cause."

After a series of warm embraces, Terence, Bridget, and Brian started walking to their gate. They hadn't gone more than seventy meters when Maeve placed both hands by the sides of her mouth and shouted through the terminal.

"Oh, me dears! I saved the best for last! Those bastards that threatened ye?" Maeve pointed to her temple with a finger pistol and dropped her thumb. "Slainte!"

Chapter Seventy-Two

ON RACE DAY, CARS AND BUSES jammed the parking lot outside Randall's Island Stadium. Above the stadium, a Goodyear blimp floated languidly, its television cameras capturing aerial images for the national ABC hookup. A banner at the entrance of the stadium proclaimed, "The 1983 AAU Open Track and Field Championship."

The infield of the stadium was a multi-ringed circus of high jumpers, long jumpers, triple jumpers, shot-putters, pole-vaulters, and hammer, javelin, and discus throwers. On the track, hurdles were set for those who ran hundred-meter hurdles. The four-hundred-meter hurdles would follow. Once the hurdles were cleared, the track was set for sprinters, middle-distance runners, then fifteen-hundred, five-thousand, and ten-thousand-meter races, and finally the steeplechase. Long-time ABC and ESPN track and field commentator Larry Rawson worked the sidelines, microphone in hand, interviewing headline runners and famous coaches. His partner, former world champion high-jumper Dwight Stones, covered competitors and coaches in the field events.

Starting guns reported every few minutes; final lap bells clanged; bodies grunted and groaned; running feet drummed; crowds shouted disappointed "ooohs and aaahs" over missed high, long, and triple jumps and pole vaults, or shouted buoyant cheers over successful ones. On the track, hurdlers, six abreast, streaked down the straightaway, stretching their legs over a high hurdle every 9.14 meters. The hurdles rattled as the runners' thighs brushed them. One runner caught his toe and fell forward, rolling over and tripping the runner to his right. Both runners required emergency help and were slow to get up.

Cooper and Benson entered the stadium wearing sunglasses, hooded sweatshirts, and sweatpants. They surveyed the field and picked up an event program. Cooper thumbed the pages.

"Here's the one I want. Begins in fifteen minutes," he said. He spotted a pair of unattended training shoes, picked them up, and walked off with them, tying the laces together and stringing them around his neck. Camouflage. He and Benson walked over to the long-jump pit, located near what would be the final turn of the eight-hundred-meter race. They sat on the infield grass, blending in with dozens of athletes warming up for their events. Cooper then gestured to a tree-shrouded, chain-link fence just beyond the pit. "Let's get on the other side of that. Better firing angle, and quick getaway from there," he said.

He and Benson relocated.

Some fifty meters from them, Tim sprinted lightly in preparation for the imminent start of his race. He was nervous today, more than at any other time in his short career. He fidgeted as he took off his sweatshirt and pants. After jogging in place for a bit, he did a few more short sprints. His singlet featured a small Irish flag and a black mourning swatch sewn onto it. As he tried to pin his racing number on his singlet, his hands shook, and he couldn't close the pin.

Blake noticed his agitation and came over.

"Here, let me do that for you." He fixed it in place. "Remember what Coach told us. These guys play tough." Tim was in a zone, barely listening. Blake continued, "Tim, I'll be by the two-hundred-meter mark again. I'll shout your splits."

Absentmindedly, he responded, "Thanks." He took two steps toward the starting line but then stopped. Turning back to Blake, he placed his hand on his neck. "I mean it Tyrone. Thank ye. For everything. Ye've helped me and taught me a lot."

Blake nodded somberly, then said, "Go win this thing."

The field announcer's voice crackled over the Randall's Island loudspeaker. "Will the runners for the 1983 AAU Open Eight-Hundred-Meter Final please report to the starting line?"

Tim jogged to the starting line and assembled with the other runners. They were given their lane assignments, and the starter issued his instructions.

"Gentlemen, the command will be 'On your mark. Set.' Then the pistol. You may not leave your lane until the 110-meter mark. Watch the pushing and tripping. We don't want any DQ's' When I call your name, I want you to step out of your lane and acknowledge the crowd. Any questions?"

There were none.

"Okay, men, let's have a great race!" The taut-faced, agitated runners shook hands with one another. Tim searched the crowd and spotted Gina in the front row of the bleachers. She smiled and waved a fist at him, then pointed to the section next to her.

"In the first lane, from the University of Oregon, last year's NCAA title holder in the mile . . . Jimmy Collins!" Collins stepped forward and waved to the crowd.

Tim scanned the crowd and noticed Gary and his Aunt Mary waving to him. Next to them were Coach Quigley and Linda.

"In the second lane, from the University of Virginia . . . "

Tim waved and patted his chest with his right hand.

"In the third lane, from Boston College, New England Eight-Hundred-Meter Champion, Willie Howard."

Howard stepped forward and offered a grandiose, theatrical arm-curling bow to the crowd. He was lustily booed.

"In the fourth lane, the exciting New York City high school runner, the Boy from Mullaghmore . . . Tim Connolly."

Tim stepped out of his lane, acknowledged the applause, and blew a two-handed kiss to his family and friends in the stands. At that moment, a small group of supporters wearing green hats and green-and-orange jackets unfurled a large banner proclaiming "The Boy from Mullaghmore."

As the announcer continued with the last competitors, Tim moved back into his lane and stared at the ground. He shook his arms and legs and did a few anxious stretches.

His face tightened into an expressionless mask. The noise around him dissolved into a dull hum. In this quiet place, the weight of events that had brought him to this moment took possession of him. This race would be different from any other. He was a messenger today, and his message could only be delivered with a victory. There was no other way.

The starter said, "Gentlemen, on your mark." The runners toed their lines. "Get set."

When all the runners were set, he fired his pistol. But a second pistol shot rang out right after, echoing through the stadium. False start. The runner from Boston College jumped too soon. "Alright gentlemen, relax. Howard, one more jump and you're out. Okay, let's try this, again."

The runners regrouped and lined up at the starting line one

more time, even more tense and anxious. Once they were set, the third pistol report produced a clean start. The runners burst off the starting line and into their lanes, their long, steady strides ranging quickly over the surface of the orange composition track. The pace of their rapidly pounding feet produced a frenetic drumbeat, bringing the crowd to its feet.

The leader, Jimmy Collins from Oregon, did not emerge until they passed the hundred-meter mark. The other runners folded in behind him from their staggered lanes, drafting off his body. Two runners "boxed" Tim in fifth place. As he tried to move to an outside lane, the runner from Virginia, tall and tautly muscled, blocked his path and threw a hard elbow into Tim's ribs. The blow interrupted his tempo, causing him to lurch forward and grimace with pain.

Watching this from the bleachers, Quigley winced and shouted. "Tim, get out of that box! Get out of that box!"

As if hearing his coach, Tim broke stride for a moment, then forced his way to the outer lane. He strode past the Virginia runner and returned a quick, sharp elbow into his solar plexus, leaving him gasping.

"Attaboy!" shouted Quigley. "Don't let the bastards push you around!"

Tim settled into fourth place. Near the two-hundred-meter mark, he saw Blake.

"Twenty-four seconds! Good pace!" shouted Blake.

Tim remained in fourth place as the pack approached the four-hundred-meter mark. As he completed it, Gina roared above the crowd.

"Forty-nine seconds! Move your ass, Greenhorn."

The bell for the final lap clanged. Suddenly, the runner from Virginia sprinted past the Oregon runner and took the lead. The Boston College runner followed him. A section of the crowd started chanting, "Mullagh-a-more! Mullagh-a-more! Mullagh-a-more!" Tim followed the Virginia and Boston College runners, passing the Oregon runner, who quickly dropped back into fifth place.

At this point in the race, an unexpected calm visited Tim. His mind transported his body into an elevated sphere, no longer feeling the weight of his footfalls, nor the sound of his measured breathing, nor the roar of the crowd. Tim was roaming the hills of his Sligo farm. The longed-for ocean breeze now lifted him above the green-gray tapestry of field, stone, and sea. Soaring and gliding like any rock-bred sea-borne bird, Tim never felt more alive, or invincible.

Just then the Virginia runner made his move down the backstretch, breaking from the pack. Tim followed him, streaking past the Boston College runner into second place, now trailing the leader by ten meters.

Blake watched Tim speeding down the back straightaway, but suddenly, from the corner of his eye, just to his right, he noticed two large figures near him pushing people aside, clearing places for themselves on the fence near the final turn. "Cooper! Benson!" He saw that Cooper held a shiny object in his right hand. It was a pistol.

Blake shouted to Tim, but his warning was lost in the crowd noise. Wildly, he bolted across the field, screaming at Tim. Still too much noise.

As Tim closed on the Virginia runner near the final turn,

Cooper's Smith & Wesson 38 Special reached over the fence, glistening in the sun. Cooper tracked Tim as he moved to the seven-hundred-meter mark and took aim and fired. A miss. The pistol's report was lost in the uproar and was largely unnoticed. Spectators at that far end of the track, however, did hear the shot and then witnessed a struggle between two large athletes, one wrestling the other to the ground.

The Virginia runner and Tim, oblivious to the off-track drama, never broke stride. Tim was now on the shoulder of his opponent with fifty meters to go. The crowd rhythmically chanted, "Mullagh-a-more, Mullagh-a-more, Mullagh-a-more!"

With thirty meters remaining, Tim moved abreast of the Virginia runner. He was breathing heavily, pumping his arms furiously. Stride for stride, they battled to the finish line. Both runners leaned desperately toward the tape. Tim's chest broke the tape.

Tim Connolly was the 1983 National AAU eight-hundred-meter champion.

The spectators roared, stomped, blew whistles and horns, clanged cowbells. As Tim staggered to a halt, he thrust his arms in the air.

He let out a maniacal scream. "Yes! Yes!" A wide grin creased his face as he pointed to his people in the bleachers. "Yes!" he shouted again before releasing a long, joyous howl. In the front row of the bleachers, Mary and Gary, along with Gina, Quigley, and Linda, cheered and celebrated. With the crowd roaring and the press and TV people rushing toward him, Tim dropped to his knees. Tears now streaming from his eyes, he covered his face and whispered.

"We did it, Da. We won. *We* won."

The crowd continued cheering as the voice from the loudspeaker announced, "Ladies and gentlemen! The winner of this year's AAU National eight-hundred-meter race, with a record-breaking time of 1:44:02, is Tim Connolly, 'The Boy from Mullaghmore!'"

Tim rose, left the track, and headed toward the front row of the bleachers, steps ahead of the reporters and cameramen in his wake.

"Tim? How's it feel to be the first high school runner in history to win this event?" shouted Marvin Stewart. "What do you have to say to your family and friends back in Ireland?

"In a few moments, please, Mr. Stewart, I'll come back and chat with all of ye," said Tim.

"Okay Tim. We'll wait here for you."

Stewart gestured to the other reporters and photographers. "Let's stay here, everybody. Give him a few moments with his family."

Chip Mullins signaled his camera crew to set up where they were.

Tim reached Quigley first and choked up. "Coach . . . I—so much . . . nothing. Nothing without you. Thank ye." He cautiously embraced his still healing Coach.

Voice full of emotion, Quigley said, "No, thank *you* son. You saved me." He took his wife's hand. Linda grabbed Tim's with her other hand and congratulated him.

Tim then reached for his aunt and uncle and tried to speak; instead, he just put his arms around them, his body, and held them. Mary and Gary muttered tearfully how proud they were of him.

Finally, Gina shouted, "Hey! What about me, Champ?"

Tim pulled her to him. "Ah, Ms. Carbone . . . the love of me life!" They joyfully hugged and kissed each other.

After a few minutes, Tim returned to the waiting reporters, who surrounded him, wielding their pencils, pads, microphones, and clicking cameras. He briskly and confidently spent ten minutes answering their questions about the race.

"One other thing," Tim said at the end. "Before ye leave, please listen, friends, and report this: I am dedicating this day, this victory, to me brave father, an innocent man, who has been unfairly imprisoned in Northern Ireland's filthy H-Block prison and brutalized with the consent of the Belfast and British governments. He has been one of the hunger strikers who has desperately tried to call attention to their terrible plight. And the world should know about him and about the human rights abuses in H-Block and the treachery of the bloody Thatcher government. I also dedicate this day—me whole life, actually—to me dear, sweet, and brave mother. She took me Da's cause to the streets and airwaves. She has helped shine a light on the cruelty of H-Block, and she has become a hero in her own right. I wish so much that they could both have been here today. Send out the word, please."

Outside the track, meanwhile, a crowd had gathered around six police officers who had Cooper and Benson in custody. Benson, handcuffed, stood calmly between two policemen, as if relieved to be in custody. He was explaining how he'd grabbed his friend's arm and lifted it just as he was about to fire. He then wrestled him to the ground to prevent him from hurting anybody. He said he was tired of being on the run, and he didn't want him or his friend to be involved in a murder. Not far from Benson, Cooper was handcuffed on his knees nearby, weeping uncontrollably, shouting.

"Shoot me. Just fuckin' shoot me!"

Blake, off to the side, was speaking with another policeman. He noticed Tim in the distance and caught his eye. Clasping his hands over his head, he shook them triumphantly. Tim laughed and returned the gesture.

As the crowd thinned out, Gary, Mary, Linda, and Coach Quigley, slowly made their way to the exit. Tim and Gina followed them. He had his arm around her waist; she had hers around his neck. She whispered in Tim's ear that she had a "special trophy" for him. He laughed, nodded enthusiastically, and pulled her even closer to him.

Chip Mullins stood in front of his TV crew and adjusted his jacket and tie.

"Are we ready to roll? Get the family over my shoulder!"

His assistant flashed a thumbs-up.

"Excitement, mayhem, and international politics at the AAU Championship today! First off, high school phenom Tim Connolly, better known as the 'Boy from Mullaghmore' won a heart-pounding eight-hundred-meter race in record time . . . "

Chapter Seventy-Three

AFTER THE RACE, MARY AND GARY hosted a celebratory lunch at their apartment. Coach Quigley was giving a cheerful post-race analysis to the group when Blake arrived, fresh from his conversation with the police. He shocked Tim and the group with the scary details of the shot fired and the arrests of Cooper and Benson. Quigley was relieved that they were finally in jail. A restrained Gina said only, "About damn time."

Then the doorbell rang. Gary had ordered cold cuts, potato salad, and macaroni salad from Rudy's Delicatessen. Rudy delivered the food himself and took a minute to congratulate Tim.

Minutes after he left, the phone rang. Gary received the call he'd been expecting and nodded knowingly several times.

"Yeah, yes, yeah. That's wonderful," he said. "We'll be there. Absolutely." He hung up. "That was Harry Perkins. He manages the parish hall. He said some big shot reserved the hall tonight to celebrate Tim's victory. He also said some well-known Irish musicians volunteered to do a trad session. One of them is the famous Joe Burke, who lives in Brooklyn now. I told them we'd be there if that's all right with everyone."

Tim loved the idea. "Joe Burke? I saw him once in Sligo with me parents."

Quigley and Linda accepted enthusiastically as well.

"Irish music?" Blake said laughing. "This will be a first for me."

"Same here," said Gina.

###

Around 8 p.m., all seven of them filed into a crowded parish hall. Tim was greeted with scattered applause. Some people came over to say hello, congratulate him, pat him on the back, or shake his hand. The hall was decorated with green, white, and orange crepe paper streamers. The homemade banner from the track meet, "The Boy from Mullaghmore," hung at the end of the hall, behind the bandstand. In front, a portable stage had been assembled. Several electricians were working on the lights—floodlights, footlights, spotlights. These were licensed technicians, not neighborhood volunteers, and they seemed intent on creating a professional set.

When the musicians arrived, they received a hearty welcome. They took their seats and casually removed their instruments from their hard-shell cases. A large Coleman cooler of chilled beer was placed next to Tommy Evans, the bodhran player, and he opened beers for each of the musicians. White-haired and bushy-bearded, Joe Burke entered the auditorium after his fellow musicians had settled in. He modestly acknowledged the audience's applause, then sat in the middle of his band. The group featured not only Joe's accordion, but also a guitar, a fiddle, two flutes, a banjo, a bagpipe, and a bodhran. They all tinkered with and tuned their instruments for a few minutes.

Once they were set, Joe tapped his feet and shouted, "One, two, three, four . . . "

The band opened with a powerful, thumping version of "O'Sullivan's March," followed by a series of high-octane jigs, hornpipes, and reels. The audience was on its feet and clapping to the intersecting flute and accordion turns, and the wild, scattering bass beat of the bodhran. After a series of fiery instrumentals, the band rested while Johnny Meagher, the banjo player, stood up and lent his fine tenor voice to several crowd favorites, like "Whiskey in the Jar," "Tim Finnegan's Wake," and "The Wild Colonial Boy," tunes that had the audience singing along.

Johnny then announced that the band was about to play "The Fields of Athenry," but first he wondered if there might be in the audience a former beauty queen from Sligo who might sing the words.

Gary proudly stood and announced, "We have such a beauty queen right here!"

Mary, flustered and embarrassed, said, "No, really Gary, I couldn't. It's been too long."

"Of course, you can, Mary. You still have a lovely voice." He took her hand and walked her to the bandstand. The audience applauded politely while Mary blushed and took several deep breaths, struggling to compose herself. The parish hall then came to a hushed silence, and the lights dimmed. Mary worked with Johnny for a few seconds to find the right key, since she had to sing now in a lower register than those many years ago. The banjo and the flute opened with a few chords, and Mary rendered a deeply personal version of what many called Ireland's unofficial national anthem.

> *By a lonely prison wall*
> *I heard a young girl calling*
> *Michael they are taking you away*
> *For you stole Trevelyan's corn*

So the young might see the morn
Now a prison ship lies waiting in the bay

Low lie the Fields of Athenry
Where once we watched the small free birds fly
Our love was on the wing
We had dreams and songs to sing
Now it's so lonely round the fields of Athenry

By a lonely prison wall
I heard a young man calling
Nothing matters Mary when you're free
Against the famine and the crown
I rebelled they cut me down
Now you must raise our child with dignity

Low lie the Fields of Athenry
Where once we watched the small free birds fly
Our love was on the wing
We had dreams and songs to sing
Now it's so lonely round the fields of Athenry

By a lonely harbor wall
She watched the last star falling
As the prison ship sailed out against the sky
Now she must live in hope and pray
For her love in Botany bay
For it's lonely round the fields of Athenry

Low lie the Fields of Athenry
Where once we watched the small free birds fly
Our love was on the wing
We had dreams and songs to sing
Now it's so lonely round the fields of Athenry.

Gary wept as Mary's keening voice touched the sorrow of this lament, the one she'd sung on the day they met and fell in love. As she sang, people in the audience began to sing the chorus with her. When it ended, Johnny took a deep bow, bowed to Mary, and then returned to his chair to spirited applause. Mary clasped her hands in front of her in a prayerful gesture as she acknowledged the applause before she left the stage.

Joe Burke then rose to speak.

"Thank you, Mrs. Laherty, for that heartfelt and beautiful rendition of 'The Fields of Athenry.' Ladies and gentlemen, it is so wonderful to be with ye tonight, and to play for ye, especially to celebrate today with this fine young Irishman . . . this championship runner, Tim Connolly."

The members of the band applauded him, and the audience joined in. Gina made Tim stand and acknowledge their support. He smiled, waved, and clapped his hands to them and the band. Joe Burke continued, "We are here also tonight to honor Tim's brave father, Terence Connolly, and his heroic mother, Bridget Connolly. Right now, in honor of this remarkable family, we have a special treat for ye. We are going to dim the lights and change the tempo for ye as we welcome two fine dancers from the west of Ireland who are going to perform a traditional two-hand dance to a favorite slip jig called 'Kitty Come Down to Limerick.'"

When the band lifted their instruments, the hall went dark except for a spotlight on the floor in front. As the music began, two dancers—a man and a woman—danced into the lighted spot. The light illuminated only their shiny black cleated shoes, rhythmically clicking and twisting on the floor. For one full minute, the audience thrilled to the dancers' rapid-fire footwork. Then the man took the woman's two hands, and they began spinning, and as they were spinning, the light slowly expanded wider and wider, and higher and higher, until it revealed their faces—the faces of Terence and Bridget Connolly.

And as they kept dancing, they gestured to their tear-stained son, Tim, to join them on stage. And he did, and he took their hands, and they danced in a circle. Together. And then they gestured to their family and friends to join them. And they did—Mary, Gary, Gina, and Blake. And the circle widened, until it finally welcomed old Brian Connolly.

And they danced.

THE END

Historical Note

ON JULY 28, 2000, THE FINAL 140 prisoners were released from Maze Prison as part of the Good Friday Agreement. In all, 428 terrorists, including 143 who were serving life sentences, were set free. Men responsible for the worst atrocities during thirty years of violence in the province, walked out and were welcomed by cheering supporters. Among them was Thomas McMahon, who had been serving a life sentence for the assassination of Lord Mountbatten. On April 18, 2021, Mary McDonald, leader of the Sinn Fein Party, apologized for the assassination of Mountbatten, saying it was "heartbreaking." She refused to apologize, however, directly to the royal family because the British army itself had committed considerable violence during the Troubles in Northern Ireland.

On September 29, 2000, Maze Prison closed its gates after almost thirty tumultuous years. Six years later, on October 30, 2006, demolition began at the former prison, and it was razed within a year. Plans to build a multipurpose sports arena on the cleared space were scrapped for lack of financial backing. Plans for a "center for conflict transformation" were also scrapped because of an unresolved conflict between Sinn Fein and the Loyalists, who worried it might become a shrine to the IRA. The barren space remains flat and undeveloped to this day, a tribute to its anguished history and "untransformed conflict."

On October 1, 2020, the Report of the Independent Panel of Inquiry into the Circumstances of the H-Block Protests 1976-

1981 concluded that there was torture, as well as inhuman and degrading treatment, and that the "ultimate legal and moral responsibility rests with the Prime Minister [Thatcher] and senior Cabinet members who knew and approved of that treatment."

Acknowledgements

SOURCE MATERIAL FOR MUCH of the cultural and historical information mentioned in this novel derives from three splendidly researched and entertaining books by Sligo's premier historian, Joe McGowan: *In the Shadow of Ben Bulben*, *A Bitter Wind*, and *Even the Heather Bled*. McGowan's work is indispensable for tracing Sligo's part in Ireland's history as well as for recording the distinctive myths and folkways of Sligo's people. Additionally, his conversation while guiding me around Mullaghmore in the summer of 2022, and his thoughtful correspondence over two years, have been invaluable aids to my work.

Shane Paul O'Doherty's *The Volunteer* and Patrick Radden Keefe's *Say Nothing* are deservedly best-selling works that offer vivid and harsh insights into the brutality and ugliness of "the Troubles." Timothy Knatchbull's *From a Clear Blue Sky* provided a heartbreaking memoir of his experience as the lone survivor of the Mountbatten bombing. Knatchbull was badly wounded, while his grandfather, grandmother, and twin brother, as well as a local friend, died in the blast. Information about Tom Barry's November 1920 Kilmichael ambush of a company of Auxiliary Division police is summarized from John Dorney's, *The Irish War of Independence, Today in Irish History*.

Close friends have been kind enough to read my story at various stages of its development and provided thoughtful and reasoned encouragement and advice.

Husband and wife Dr. Barbara Baines, Professor Emerita, NC State University and Dr. Leigh De Neef, Professor Emeritus, Duke University generously supported me from the very beginning, and gently offered suggestions and opinions that pointed me in the right direction.

Dr. Mary Helen Thuente, Professor Emerita, NC State University, and former English Department Head, helpfully warned me away from specific excesses, especially in my early enthusiasm for banshees.

Dr. Mike Scully, retired pediatric surgeon and undergraduate classmate and fellow track teammate at Boston College, reminded me of things about the art and science of running that I had forgotten. Pat McCall is an old friend and fellow Master's Track teammate from our days with the Syracuse Chargers Track Club. Pat's stories from his Roscommon family inspired much of the humor in my story. In gratitude to both Pat and Mike, I named two of my favorite characters after them.

Dr. Barry Monahan, Professor of Film Studies at University College Cork, partnered with me on my two final study tours of Ireland with American college students. His teaching and mentoring made the summer program a success for our students. His intelligence, generosity, and good humor have made him one of my dearest friends. Furthermore, Barry's enthusiastic reading of my manuscript encouraged me with the sense that the work passed muster with a Cork man.

Frank Bard Young, an old friend from graduate school and fellow editor on the *Milton Quarterly*, employed his skills as former editor of Vanderbilt University Press by giving my manuscript a no-nonsense assessment of a near-final draft that effectively spun me in a decidedly more productive direction.

Most of all, my extraordinary, wise, and beautiful wife, Connie Kretchmar, was instrumental in getting this story finished. A tireless reader and shrewd critic, Connie thoughtfully and patiently proofread my chapters with expert and careful attention.